STUDY GUIDE AND WORKBOOK

Music

second edition

Daniel T. Politoske
University of Kansas

Prentice-Hall, Inc.

Englewood Cliffs, N.J.

ISBN 0-13-607564-9

Printed in the United States of America

10 9 8 7 6 5 4 3 2 1

Prentice-Hall International, Inc., London
Prentice-Hall of Australia Pty. Ltd., Sydney
Prentice-Hall of Canada, Ltd., Toronto
Prentice-Hall of India Private Limited, New Delhi
Prentice-Hall of Japan, Inc., Tokyo
Prentice-Hall of Southeast Asia Pte. Ltd., Singapore
Whitehall Books Limited, Wellington, New Zealand

Contents

Preface

The <u>Study Guide and Workbook</u> that accompanies the Second Edition of MUSIC has been designed as an aid to your study of our musical heritage. In each chapter you will find three sections:

1. <u>Key Terms and Concepts</u>. The outlines given at the beginning of each chapter can be used both as a preview of the material to be studied and later as a checklist for review.

2. <u>Self-Tests</u>. These twenty-item tests covering the most important aspects in each chapter will allow you to check your grasp of the ideas presented.

3. <u>Directed Listening</u>. The listening questions found at the end of each chapter are designed to guide you in listening for specific elements in the works included in the record set that accompanies the text.

Also included in the <u>Study Guide and Workbook</u> are seven <u>Cumulative Reviews</u>. Each will serve to reinforce material covered in earlier chapters and offer points of comparison that will allow you to see the music of the past in a much broader framework. Each review contains two sections:

1. <u>Cumulative Review Self-Tests</u>. In these twenty-item tests you will be asked to identify particular periods and to review the most important concepts and terms associated with them.

2. <u>Cumulative Review Directed Listening</u>. The questions in these sections call for comparison of works from different periods--comparisons based not only on your increasing factual understanding but also on your enhanced ability to. listen to music with care and sensitivity.

Before you read any of the questions in the <u>Self-Tests</u> and <u>Directed Listening</u> sections, take a sheet of paper and cover the answers that appear in the half-brackets on the right side of the page. Write the answers to the questions in the spaces provided on the page and then check your answers with the correct ones.

The material presented in the <u>Study Guide and Workbook</u> will be as useful as you will let it be. Use it to help you review the factual information that will, in turn, help you derive more from your listening experiences. And, above all, enjoy your listening experiences.

ACKNOWLEDGMENTS

Special thanks are due to Carol Berger for her assistance in the preparation of the revised <u>Study Guide and Workbook</u> and to the project editor, Stephanie Roby.

I
Melody and Rhythm

KEY TERMS AND CONCEPTS

SELF-TEST

Completion Questions:

1. The _____ of any musical tone is
   determined by the number of vibrations
   per second.   [pitch

2. A succession of tones used in a meaningful,
   expressive way is called a _____.   [melody

3. A melody in which there are wide distances
   or leaps between the successive tones is
   called a _____ melody.   [disjunct

4. A _____ is one small section of the   [phrase
   melody, corresponding roughly to one line of
   an entire poem.

5. The term _____ is used to describe the   [rhythm
   organization of music in time.

6. The pattern of accented and unaccented beats
   in music is called _____.   [meter

7. If we hear beats in groups of two we say that
   the music is in _____ meter.   [duple

8. Small and generally consistent groups of strong
   and weak beats are organized into _____.   [measures

9. The overall speed at which a composer directs
   a composition to be played is called the
   _____.   [tempo

10. A temporary slowing down of the speed at
    which a piece is played is indicated by a
    _____.   [ritardando

Multiple Choice:

11. The highest tone of a piano or violin is
    produced by the string that vibrates
    a. the least rapidly.
    b. the most rapidly.
    c. at roughly twice the speed of the lowest
       string.   [b

2

12. When a strong accent recurs on the first
    beat of each group of three beats, we may
    say that the piece is in
    a. march time.
    b. waltz time.
    c. ragtime.   [b

13. In syncopation
    a. an accented tone is sounded on a
       normally weak beat.
    b. a tone is sung a half tone lower than
       usual.
    c. the melody is repeated in shortened form.   [a

True or False:

14. Our ear can usually supply the tone at which
    a given melody will come to rest.   [true

15. Composers generally try to avoid repeating
    any melodic or rhythmic material.   [false

Matching:

16. Very slow   ____ andante   [19
17. Very fast   ____ allegro   [18
18. Fast   ____ vivace   [17
19. Moderate   ____ largo   [16
20. Slow   ____ adagio   [20

DIRECTED LISTENING

1. The melody at the beginning of Richard
   Strauss's Till Eulenspiegels lustige Streiche
   (Side 8, Band 2) is made up of
   a. ascending tones.
   b. descending tones.   [a

2. The melody at the beginning of the first
   movement of Mozart's Symphony No. 40 in G
   Minor (Side 4, Band 3) is prominently
   a. conjunct.
   b. disjunct.   [a

3

3. Which of the following rhythmic patterns
   fits the "Promenade" in Mussorgsky's <u>Pictures</u>
   <u>at an Exhibition</u> (Side 9, Band 3)?
   a. — —— — —— — — —
   b. —— — — —— — —
   c. — —— —— — — —   [c

4. The pattern of beats in Morley's "Now Is
   the Month of Maying" (Side 2, Band 12) is in
   a. duple meter.
   b. triple meter.   [a

5. The tempos in the first two sections of
   Copland's <u>Appalachian Spring</u> (Side 11, Band
   2) are best described as
   a. moderato--presto--grave.
   b. largo--vivace--adagio.
   c. andante--allegro--vivace.   [b

2
Harmony and Texture

KEY TERMS AND CONCEPTS

Harmony
  Sound Relationships
    Intervals and Chords
    Octave
  Scales
    Chromatic
    Major and Minor
  Triads
    Tonic Chord
    Subdominant and Dominant Chords
  Cadences
    Resolution
    Authentic and Plagal
  Harmonic Perception
    Consonance and Dissonance
  Changes in Tonality
    Accidentals and Modulation
Texture
  Monophony
  Polyphony or Counterpoint
  Homophony

SELF-TEST

Completion Questions:

1. _____ is the sounding together of two
   or more tones.   [Harmony

2. The distance between two tones is referred
   to as an _____.   [interval

3. Three or more tones played simultaneously
   are called a _____.   [chord

4. On the keyboard, two tones separated by
   exactly eight white keys are known as an
   _____.   [octave

5. The successive sounding of all the black and
   white keys between two notes an octave apart
   produces what is known as the _____ scale.   [chromatic

6. Most music is based not on the chromatic scale
   but rather on the familiar-sounding _____
   scale.   [major

7. There are _____ different tones in a
   major or minor scale.   [seven

8. Chords that are generally pleasing to the ear
   can be described as _____.   [consonant

9. A note not found in a composition's basic
   scale, but which is used in the composition,
   is called an _____.   [accidental

10. The interaction of musical sounds, or lines
    of sound, in a composition is referred to as
    _____.   [texture

Multiple Choice:

11. In any major scale, the tone that conveys
    rest and finality is called the
    a. dominant.
    b. subdominant.
    c. tonic.   [c

6

12. A chord constructed from three alternate
    tones in a major scale is called
    a. a cadence.
    b. a resolution.
    c. a triad.   [c

13. The I chord is the chord constructed on the
    a. tonic note of the scale.
    b. dominant note of the scale.
    c. supertonic note of the scale.   [a

14. The chord that leads most strongly to the I
    chord is the
    a. V chord.
    b. IV chord.
    c. VI chord.   [a

15. The term "authentic cadence" describes the
    chordal progression from
    a. V to I.
    b. IV to I.
    c. I to V.   [a

16. A change of tonality during a composition is
    called
    a. a modulation.
    b. a dissonance.
    c. an accidental.   [a

17. In Western music, texture
    a. is always constant throughout a
       composition.
    b. usually changes once within a composition.
    c. is not always constant throughout a
       composition.   [c

Matching:

18. A girl playing a   ___ polyphony   [19
    melody on a flute   ___ monophony   [18
19. A round with all the   ___ homophony   [20
    voices in motion
20. A baritone singing a
    solo with chordal piano
    accompaniment

DIRECTED LISTENING

1. The first six notes of the second
   movement of Haydn's Symphony No. 94 in
   G Major (Side 4, Band 2) are made up
   of which tones of the major scale?
   a. Do-re-mi
   b. Do-mi-sol
   c. Do-fa-ti   [b

2. The scale upon which Schubert's "Gute Nacht"
   (Side 7, Band 3) is based is
   a. major.
   b. minor.
   c. chromatic.   [b

3. The opening choral lines of Handel's
   "For Unto Us a Child Is Born" (Side 3,
   Band 7) produce a texture that is
   a. monophonic.
   b. polyphonic.
   c. homophonic.   [b

4. Which terms apply to Schumann's "Widmung"
   (Side 7, Band 4)?
   a. Polyphonic--consonant
   b. Homophonic--dissonant
   c. Homophonic--consonant   [c

5. The texture of which of the following pieces
   is best represented by the graph below?
   a. Monteverdi's "Tu se' morta" (Side 3,
      Band 5)
   b. Introit of the Requiem Mass (Side 2,
      Band 5)
   c. Bach's Fugue in G Minor (Side 3,
      Band 4)   [a

8

3
Timbre and Dynamics

KEY TERMS AND CONCEPTS

Timbre
  Vocal
    Soprano, Mezzo-Soprano, Contralto
    Tenor, Baritone, Bass
  Instrumental
    String Instruments (Chordophones)
      Bowed, Plucked, Strummed
    Wind Instruments (Aerophones)
      Woodwinds and Brass
    Percussion Instruments (Idiophones and Membranophones)
    Keyboard Instruments
    Older and More Recent Instruments
      Recorder and Oboe D'Amore
      Sound Synthesizer
Orchestra
  Orchestration
Dynamics
  Crescendo and Decrescendo

SELF-TEST

Completion Questions:

1. The vocal chords can be shortened to
   produce _____ pitches.   [higher

2. The tone quality of instruments or voices
   is known as _____.   [timbre

3. Instruments that produce sound through the
   vibration of strings are technically
   classified as _____.   [chordophones

4. The lowest-pitched string instrument in the
   orchestra is the _____.   [double bass

5. The type of instrument in which a player
   forces breath through a tube and thus
   causes a column of air to vibrate is
   technically known as an _____.   [aerophone

6. Some woodwinds, such as the clarinet, are
   equipped with flexible _____, which   [reeds
   vibrate when the instrument is played.

7. Percussion instruments include both _____,   [idiophones
   such as gongs, in which the whole body of
   the instrument vibrates, and membranophones,
   in which a membrane or drum head vibrates.

8. Tones are produced on the piano when small
   _____ strike a series of carefully tuned   [hammers
   strings.

9. Today's symphony orchestra is generally
   divided into four sections: strings,
   woodwinds, _____, and percussion.   [brasses

10. _____ markings indicate the level of   [Dynamic
    volume at which a composer intends a certain
    passage to be played.

Multiple Choice:

11. Instruments are divided into families
    according to their
    a. color and size.
    b. basic shape and quality.
    c. means of producing sound.   [c

12. Chordophones specifically designed to be
    plucked or strummed include the
    a. guitar, flute, and viola.
    b. banjo, cello, and viola.
    c. guitar, banjo, and ukulele.   [c

13. Usually, a new instrument
    a. can play louder than its predecessor.
    b. extends the technical capacities of
       its predecessor.
    c. is regarded with disfavor by most
       composers.   [b

True or False:

14. The double-reed orchestral instruments
    include the oboe, French horn, bassoon,
    and contra-bassoon.   [false

15. Valves in the horns are used to make the
    vibrating air column wider or narrower,
    thus changing the pitch.   [false

Matching:

16. Very loud   ___ mezzo piano   [20
17. A gradual increase   ___ pianissimo   [18
    of sound   ___ crescendo   [17
18. Very soft   ___ fortissimo   [16
19. A gradual decrease   ___ diminuendo   [19
    of sound
20. Moderately soft

DIRECTED LISTENING

1. In Davidovsky's "Synchronisms No. 1"
   (Side 12, Band 2), many unconventional
   sounds are created by a sound synthesizer.
   What wind instrument is heard playing
   along with the synthesizer?
   a. Flute
   b. Oboe
   c. Trombone   [a

2. At the beginning of Mussorgsky's Pictures
   at an Exhibition (Side 9, Band 3), the
   sound is a blend of what two orchestral
   sections?
   a. Woodwinds and strings
   b. Brass and strings
   c. Brass and percussion   [b

3. The instrument heard in Scarlatti's Sonata
   in C Major (Side 3, Band 1) is
   a. a harpsichord.
   b. a piano.
   c. an organ.   [a

4. In the opening phrases of the second
   movement of Haydn's Symphony No. 94 in G
   Major (Side 4, Band 2), the dynamics change
   from
   a. forte to piano to mezzo piano.
   b. piano to pianissimo to fortissimo.   [b

5. The last measures of the third movement of
   Tchaikovsky's Violin Concerto in D Major
   (Side 8, Band 1) offer a good example of
   a. $>$.
   b. $\boldsymbol{fp}$.
   c. $<$.   [c

4

Introduction to Musical Form and Style

KEY TERMS AND CONCEPTS

Organizational Elements of Musical Form
  Repetition and Contrast
  Motives and Phrases
  Sections and Movements
Common Forms
  Strophic
  Ternary
  Binary
  Theme and Variations
Types of Compositions
  Single-Form and Multiple-Form Works
Musical Style
  Medieval, Renaissance, Baroque
  Classical, Romantic, Twentieth Century

SELF-TEST

Completion Questions:

1. In music, the overall design of a
   composition is called the _____.   [form

2. Two fundamental principles of musical form are repetition and _____.   [contrast

3. The first eight lines of "The Star-Spangled Banner" make up two identical _____.   [sections

4. The entire composition known as "The Star-Spangled Banner" is made up of four identical _____.   [stanzas

5. Frequently, the _____ section of a work written in ternary form offers a contrast to the other sections.   [second

6. _____, such as those of Haydn and Mozart, are examples of ternary form.   [Minuets

7. Often the second section of a work written in binary form is designed to _____ the first.   [answer

8. Often a composer wishes to state one musical idea and then offer a series of elaborations on this one theme. This form is known as _____.   [theme and variations

9. Two elaborate forms developed in the eighteenth century are the _____ and rondo forms.   [sonata

10. A symphony is made up of a number of _____.   [movements

Multiple Choice:

11. Usually, a musical composition is best understood and enjoyed if
    a. it can be related to recognizable sounds of nature or human activity.
    b. the listener has some training as a performer.
    c. the listener can perceive how patterns of sound in different parts of it are related to one another.   [c

12. The two most fundamental principles of
    musical form are
    a. repetition and contrast.
    b. theme and variations.
    c. clarity and balance.   [a

13. In the round "Frère Jacques," each short
    motive is repeated
    a. twice.
    b. once.
    c. not at all.   [a

14. The form of "Frère Jacques" can be analyzed
    as
    a. ababab.
    b. aabbccdd.
    c. ABA.   [b

15. Ternary form indicates that a composition
    is written in
    a. two distinct sections.
    b. one long, uninterrupted movement.
    c. three distinct sections.   [c

16. If a composition has two distinct sections,
    it is said to be in
    a. binary form.
    b. dual form.
    c. strophic form.   [a

Matching:

17. Binary form   ___ I II III   [20
18. Ternary form   ___ ABA   [18
19. Theme and variations   ___ A – A^1– A^2– A^3– A^4 [19
20. Strophic form   ___ AB   [17

DIRECTED LISTENING

1. Liszt's Hungarian Rhapsody No. 6 (Side 7,
   Band 2) is made up of _____ sections,
   most obviously marked by changes in tempo.
   a. three
   b. four
   c. five   [b

2. The first movement of Beethoven's <u>Symphony No. 5 in C Minor</u> (Side 5, Band 1) is based largely on variations of a single motive. Which graphic representation best fits this motive?
   a. — — — —
   b. — — — —
   c. — — — —   [c

3. The form of Schubert's "Gute Nacht" (Side 7, Band 3) is
   a. strophic.
   b. binary.
   c. ternary.   [a

4. The form of Schumann's "Widmung" (Side 7, Band 4) is
   a. strophic.
   b. binary.
   c. ternary.   [c

5. Which letter designation best fits Josquin's Kyrie of the <u>Missa pange lingua</u> (Side 2, Band 9)?
   a. ABC
   b. ABA
   c. ABB   [a

5
Musical Notation

KEY TERMS AND CONCEPTS

Pitch
  Staff and Great Staff
    Ledger Lines
  Clef
    Treble (G) and Bass (F)
    Alto and Tenor (C)
  Symbols Modifying Pitch
    Sharps and Flats
    Accidentals and Natural Signs
Key
  Key Signature
  Major and Relative Minor Scales
  Major and Minor Modes
Duration
  Note Values
  Symbols Modifying Duration
    Ties and Dots
  Rests
Meter
  Measures and Bar Lines
  Time Signature
    Common and Cut Time

SELF-TEST

Completion Questions:

1. Fundamentally, musical notation is designed
   to indicate two things: pitch and _____   [duration
   of the musical tones.

2. The pitch of a note is shown by its vertical
   location on a series of horizontal lines
   called a _____.   [staff

3. The sign that appears at the extreme left of
   the staff, indicating the pitch represented
   by the various lines and spaces, is called
   a _____.   [clef

4. The most familiar clef is the _____ or   [treble
   G clef.

5. The notes of the black keys on the piano are
   shown through the use of _____ and flat   [sharp
   signs.

6. The _____ signature shows which notes will [key
   be sharped or flatted throughout a piece of
   music.

7. Each major scale shares its seven basic tones
   with a _____ minor scale.   [relative

8. A _____ signature is given next to the   [time
   key signature at the beginning of the piece.

9. If a whole note represents four beats, a
   half note will represent _____ beats.   [two

10. Periods of silence in music are notated by
    _____ signs.   [rest

Multiple Choice:

11. Reading music is the process of
    a. translating notes into written language.
    b. memorizing a set of fixed pitches.
    c. translating written symbols into
       equivalent sounds.   [c

18

12. The modern staff consists of
    a. three lines.
    b. four lines.
    c. five lines.   [c

13. Performers know they must raise the pitch
    of a particular note by a half step when
    they see a
    a. sharp sign.
    b. flat sign.
    c. natural sign.   [a

14. When a particular note is to be sharped or
    flatted throughout a piece, the composer
    a. writes a sharp or flat beside the
       note each time it occurs.
    b. places the sharp or flat sign for the
       note immediately after the clef.
    c. changes the composition to a less complex
       key.   [b

15. A natural sign might occur after a particular
    note has been
    a. sharped or flatted.
    b. prolonged.
    c. played in the octave above.   [a

16. In $\frac{2}{4}$ time
    a. the quarter note has a value of one beat
       and there are two beats in a measure.
    b. the half note has a value of one beat and
       there are four beats in a measure.
    c. neither of the above.   [a

Match the pairs of notes that are written
differently but would sound the same on the
piano.

17. A♯   ____ D♭   [20
18. F♯   ____ A♭   [19
19. G♯   ____ G♭   [18
20. C♯   ____ B♭   [17

DIRECTED LISTENING

1. The vocal part of Verdi's "Ah, fors' è lui"
   (Side 8, Band 3) is most likely written on
   a staff with a
   a. treble clef.
   b. alto clef.
   c. bass clef.   [a

2. Chopin's Nocturne in E♭ Major (Side 7, Band 1)
   would be written on a
   a. five-line staff.
   b. great staff.
   c. chromatic staff.   [b

3. Which sign of duration is prominently used
   in the opening measures of vocal music in
   Mozart's The Marriage of Figaro (Side 6,
   Band 4)?
   a. Rest
   b. Tie
   c. Dot   [a

4. The time signature of the first movement of
   Beethoven's String Quartet No. 7 in F Major
   (Side 6, Band 3) is
   a. $\frac{3}{4}$.
   b. $\frac{4}{4}$.   [b

5. Which of the following pieces would more likely
   be written with an alla breve time signature?
   a. Debussy's Prélude à l'après-midi d'un faune
      (Side 9, Band 4)
   b. Third movement of Tchaikovsky's Violin
      Concerto in D Major (Side 8, Band 1)   [b

Cumulative Review
The Elements of Music

Matching:

1. Allegro	___ woodwind	[4
2. 4/4	___ meter	[5
3. Crescendo	___ tempo	[1
4. Flute	___ ternary form	[7
5. Duple	___ cadence	[9
6. Repetition and	___ dynamics	[3
contrast	___ time signature	[2
7. ABA	___ melodic structure	[6
8. Counterpoint	___ polyphony	[8
9. V-I	___ chordophone	[10
10. Double bass		

Completion Questions:

11. A melody that moves in small tonal steps
    is called a _____ melody.   [conjunct

12. It seems natural to expect a melody to
    end on the _____ note.   [tonic

13. The plagal cadence is the progression from
    the _____ chord to the tonic chord.   [subdominant

14. A time signature of $\frac{3}{8}$ shows that there are
    _____ beats to a measure.   [three

15. A work in two distinct sections is in
    _____ form.   [binary

16. Dynamic markings indicate the level of
    _____ at which a certain passage should   [volume
    be played.

17. A sharp sign tells a performer to _____   [raise
    the pitch of a particular note by a half step.

18. In much Western music, beats are arranged
    in regular groups of equal length, with the
    accent usually falling on the _____ beat of   [first
    each group.

19. A gradual increase of sound is called a _____.   [crescendo

20. A _____ texture consists of a single   [monophonic
    melodic line without accompaniment.

DIRECTED LISTENING

1. Which of these pieces has a tempo that could
   be marked lento?
   a. Morley's "Now Is the Month of Maying" (Side
      2, Band 12)
   b. Palestrina's Kyrie of the Missa brevis
      (Side 2, Band 10)   [b

2. Dynamics play an important dramatic role in
   a. Machaut's "Douce dame jolie" (Side 2, Band 8).
   b. the first movement of Mozart's Symphony No.
      40 in G Minor (Side 4, Band 3).   [b

3. Which piece makes the greatest use of homophony?
   a. The first movement of Bach's Cantata No.
      80 (Side 3, Band 6)
   b. Chopin's Nocturne in E♭ Major (Side 7,
      Band 1)   [b

4. The melodic tones of the opening measures of
   the first movement of Brahms' Symphony No. 3
   in F Major (Side 7, Band 5) are
   a. ascending.
   b. descending.   [a

22

6
Music in Other Cultures

KEY TERMS AND CONCEPTS

Africa
  Responsorial Singing
  Harmonic Techniques
    Parallel Motion, Imitation, Drone Note
  Rhythmic Polyphony
American Indian
  Plains-Pueblo Region
    Wide Pitch Range and Descending Motion
    Incomplete Repetition
    Tense Voice Quality
  Eskimo-Northwest Coast Region
    Undulating Melodies
    Recitative Style
    Rudimentary Part Singing
India
  Ragas and Talas
  Drone Note or Chord
  Improvisation
China
  Ya-yueh and Su-yueh Music
  Pentatonic Scales
  Chinese Opera
Japan
  Gagaku
  Elastic Rhythm
  Theatre Music
    Noh Drama, Kabuki Plays, Bunraku

SELF-TEST

Completion Questions:

1. In most Bantu languages, the meaning of a word depends, in part, on the _____ at which it is spoken.   [pitch

2. In Bantu ensemble playing, rhythmic patterns in several different meters may be used simultaneously in a sort of rhythmic _____.   [polyphony

3. The best-known music of the Pueblos is that of the _____ dances.   [Kachina

4. Northwest Coast music differs from all other American Indian music in that it includes rudimentary _____.   [part singing

5. In India, melodic possibilities are explored through melodic formulas, which are known as _____.   [ragas

6. Indian music also makes use of rhythmic formulas, known as _____.   [talas

7. The two basic types of Chinese music are the _____ and the su-yueh.   [ya-yueh

8. The Chinese developed a system of written _____ quite early.   [notation

9. In their music, the Japanese were highly influenced by the music of _____.   [China

10. Japanese ensembles tend to be _____ than their Chinese counterparts.   [smaller

True or False:

11. In Bantu responsorial singing, singer and instrumentalist alternate in an improvisational contest.   [false

12. There is very little emphasis on rhythm in African music.   [false

24

13. Plains melodies cover a wide pitch range,
    beginning quite high and moving downward.   [true

14. A distinctive characteristic of Pueblo
    singing is the preference for a low, growling
    vocal style.   [true

Multiple Choice:

15. Early musicians in India believed that
    a. correct performance helped to harmonize
       the universe.
    b. the god Krishna invented the first scale.
    c. music must be performed only in the evening.   [a

16. Since Indian musical theory stresses that all
    notes derive their meaning and effect from
    their relation to the tonic
    a. the tonic chord is sounded at the beginning
       of each measure.
    b. the listener must keep the tonic chord con-
       stantly in mind.
    c. a drone on the tonic is often played through-
       out the raga.   [c

17. Chinese instruments are classified according
    to the
    a. dynastic period in which they were invented.
    b. material from which they are made.
    c. volume of sound they can produce.   [b

18. Chinese music does not use
    a. written notation.
    b. chordal harmony.
    c. percussive instruments.   [b

19. A distinctly Japanese element is the use of
    a. elastic, or breath, rhythm.
    b. strongly accented meter.
    c. subtly varied harmonies.   [a

20. Three well-known Japanese theatrical forms in
    which music plays a large part are
    a. noh, bunraku, and Peking.
    b. noh, kabuki, and bunraku.
    c. Canton, Peking, and kabuki.   [b

DIRECTED LISTENING

"Work Song from Burundi" (Side 2, Band 1)

1. The timbre in this work consists of
   a. voices and drums.
   b. voices only.
   c. voices, drums, and string instruments.
   d. voices and string instruments.   [b

2. The singing is divided between
   a. men and women.
   b. two groups of equal size.
   c. a leader and a chorus.
   d. a leader and an answering soloist.   [c

3. Each phrase sung by the leader is answered by
   a. a short melodic motive.
   b. a lengthy refrain.
   c. a repetition of the same phrase.
   d. a wordless rhythmic motive.   [a

4. The leader
   a. repeats a cycle of three phrases.
   b. often repeats the same phrase.
   c. introduces a new phrase each time he sings.
   d. alternates new phrases with repetitions of
      the opening phrase.   [b

"Ibihubi" (Side 2, Band 2)

1. The timbre in this work consists of
   a. voices and drums.
   b. voices alone.
   c. drums alone.
   d. drums and other percussion instruments.   [c

2. The musical element of the greatest interest
   here is
   a. melody.
   b. texture.
   c. harmony.
   d. rhythm.   [d

3. The complexity of the sound results from
   a. the wide variety of instrumental timbres.
   b. the different rhythmic patterns played by each instrument.
   c. subtly overlapping harmonies.
   d. the melodic use of percussion instruments.   [b

4. The texture, with its different rhythms proceeding simultaneously, could be called
   a. polyphonic.
   b. homophonic.
   c. monophonic.
   d. syncopated.   [a

"Sioux Sun Dance" (Side 2, Band 3)

1. The melodic motion of each phrase starts with a high note and then
   a. moves downward through a series of short, rather jagged steps.
   b. moves upward through a series of smooth slides.
   c. maintains an almost unvarying pitch level.   [a

2. For the most part, the voices sing in
   a. four-part harmony.
   b. unison.
   c. parallel thirds.   [b

3. The song is developed through
   a. dissonant harmonies.
   b. contrasting phrases.
   c. melodic repetition.   [c

4. The drum beat
   a. never varies.
   b. becomes slower and louder.
   c. becomes faster and softer.   [b

Section of the Noh Drama Hagaromo (Side 2, Band 4)

1. The basic timbre consists of
   a. voices alone.
   b. voices and drums.
   c. voices and string instruments.
   d. voices and a wind instrument.   [b

2. The singers' melodic line consists of
   a. a lyrical melody in a narrow range.
   b. constant scale passages.
   c. repeated notes combined with large skips.
   d. a duplication of the instrumental pattern.   [c

3. The singers fall into the Western voice
   category of
   a. soprano.
   b. alto.
   c. tenor.
   d. baritone.   [d

4. The instrument heard briefly entering and
   leaving passages of the singing is a
   a. harpsichord.
   b. small string instrument.
   c. flute.
   d. oboe.   [c

7
Medieval Music

KEY TERMS AND CONCEPTS

Monophonic Religious Music
   Settings of the Mass
     Proper and Ordinary Texts
     Plainchant or Gregorian Chant
   Eight Church Modes
     Authentic and Plagal Versions
   Neumes
   Melodic Styles
     Melismatic, Syllabic, Neumatic
   Hymns
Early Secular Music
   Troubadours, Trouvères, Minnesingers
Growth of Polyphony
   Parallel Organum
   Tenor and Duplum Lines
   Organum and Discantus Styles
   Motet Combining Secular and Religious Texts
Music of the Fourteenth Century
   Rhythmic Innovations
     Use of Duple Meter
     Isorhythm
     Rhythmic Complexity
   French Forms
     Rondeau, Virelai, Ballade, Lai
   Italian Forms
     Madrigal, Caccia, Ballata
   Exact Imitation

SELF-TEST

Completion Questions:

1. During the Dark Ages, the church distrusted "pagan" music and banned the use of musical _____ in public worship.

    [instruments

2. The liturgy for the Mass consists of two main parts: the Ordinary, for which the text is always the same but the music may vary; and the _____, in which text and music both change according to the day.

    [Proper

3. The early music written for the Mass is called _____.

    [plainchant

4. Plainchant consists of a single melodic line, sung by a soloist or unison choir without _____.

    [accompaniment

5. Songs of courtly love were written in the luxurious courts of southern France by poet-musicians called _____.

    [troubadours

6. The earliest type of polyphony was called _____.

    [organum

7. A great twelfth-century choirmaster and composer named _____ worked at the Cathedral of Notre Dame in Paris.

    [Leonin

8. His music, collected in a volume called the Magnus liber organi, is written in two styles of two-part polyphony--organum and _____.

    [discantus

9. By the end of the thirteenth century, the tenor line of many motets was no longer taken from plainchant but from _____ songs.

    [secular

10. Philippe de Vitry used the term _____ as the title for his treatise on new fourteenth-century music.

    [ars nova

Multiple Choice:

11. Melismatic plainchant was written with
    a. one note per syllable.
    b. one to three notes per syllable.
    c. many notes per syllable.   [c

12. Plainchant melodies were written in modes
    based on a system derived from
    a. Hebrew folksongs.
    b. the ancient Greeks.
    c. Arabic notation.   [b

13. These modes each occurred in two versions:
    a. the authentic and the plagal.
    b. the major and the minor.
    c. the tonal and the chromatic.   [a

14. Plainchant was notated in symbols called
    a. neumes.
    b. motets.
    c. syllabics.   [a

15. In the earliest type of organum
    a. the second voice wove an elaborate melisma
       around the original line.
    b. the organ played parallel to the voice
       line.
    c. the two voices moved in parallel motion.   [c

16. The tenor line came to be called such because
    a. it was the lowest voice.
    b. its notes were stretched out to great
       length, while the upper voices moved more
       quickly.
    c. it was kept in Latin, even when the other
       voices were in the vernacular.   [b

17. In discantus style, the tenor line moves
    a. more slowly than in organum style.
    b. more quickly than in organum style.
    c. exactly parallel to the duplum line.   [b

18. During the fourteenth century, the Church
    a. expressed concern over the growing
       elaboration of liturgical music.
    b. temporarily forbade the use of plainchant.
    c. reorganized the liturgy.   [a

19. A significant development in rhythm around the beginning of the fourteenth century was that
    a. regular meter was introduced.
    b. duple meter became as acceptable as triple meter.
    c. duple meter began to replace triple meter.   [b

20. The only complete fourteenth-century setting of the Ordinary by one composer is the <u>Messe de Nostre Dame</u> by
    a. Bernart de Ventadorn.
    b. Philippe de Vitry.
    c. Guillaume de Machaut.   [c

DIRECTED LISTENING

Introit of the Requiem Mass (Side 2, Band 5)

1. Melodic movement is mainly
   a. conjunct.
   b. disjunct.
   c. upward.
   d. downward.   [a

2. Both the text and the music of the Introit are in an
   a. AB form.
   b. ABA form.
   c. ABC form.
   d. ABAC form.   [b

3. The relationship of text to melody is mainly
   a. melismatic.
   b. syllabic.
   c. neumatic.   [c

4. Which of the following elements is <u>not</u> present?
   a. Monophonic texture
   b. Tenor voices
   c. Dynamic changes   [c

Ventadorn: "Be m'an perdut" (Side 2, Band 6)

1. The texture of the song is
   a. homophonic.
   b. monophonic.
   c. polyphonic.   [b

2. The meter is
   a. duple.
   b. triple.
   c. irregular.   [b

3. The first melody is
   a. repeated several times.
   b. heard once at the beginning and once at
      the end.
   c. used only at the beginning of the song.   [a

4. Timbre consists of
   a. a single voice.
   b. voice and harp.
   c. voice and drum.   [a

Leonin: Viderunt omnes (Side 2, Band 7)

1. At the beginning, the lower voice or tenor
   moves
   a. in a series of long, drawn-out notes.
   b. in exact duplication with the upper voice.
   c. in parallel thirds with the upper voice.   [a

2. The tenor voice
   a. sometimes disappears temporarily.
   b. occasionally quickens its motion in
      discantus style.
   c. maintains throughout the slow motion
      characteristic of organum style.   [b

3. The melodic movement of the duplum or top
   voice is
   a. exactly parallel to the tenor.
   b. syllabic.
   c. highly melismatic and decorative.   [c

4. The texture of the work is
   a. entirely polyphonic.
   b. polyphonic and homophonic.
   c. polyphonic and monophonic.   [c

Machaut: "Douce dame jolie" (Side 2, Band 8)

1. The texture of this song is basically
   a. homophonic.
   b. polyphonic.
   c. monophonic.
   d. imitative.   [c

2. The song is organized into
   a. three sections, interspersed with a refrain.
   b. sections of irregular length, each repeated
      twice.
   c. four sections without repetition.
   d. two sections repeated in a certain pattern.   [d

3. The meter is
   a. duple.
   b. triple.
   c. variable.
   d. isorhythmic.   [a

4. The recorder doubles the voice
   a. exactly note-for-note.
   b. in organum style.
   c. in discantus style.
   d. at an interval of a fifth.   [a

8
Renaissance Music

KEY TERMS AND CONCEPTS

New Developments in Polyphony
  Four-Part Texture
  Careful Use of Dissonance
  Wide Use of Imitation
  Text Painting
Religious Music
  Fifteenth-Century Motet
  Use of Canon
  Paraphrase Technique
  Chorale
Secular Music
  Frottola and Chanson
  Sixteenth-Century Italian Madrigal
  English Madrigal, Ballett, and Ayre
Instrumental Music
  Consorts and Broken Consorts
  Recorders, Viols, Lutes, Organ, Harpsichord
  Instrumental Dances
    Pavane and Galliard
  Instrumental Pieces
    Ricercar, Fantasia, Canzona

SELF-TEST

Completion Questions:

1. By the middle of the Renaissance, most choral
   works were written in _____ parts.   [four

2. During the Renaissance, dissonance was
   reserved for special effects, dramatic moments
   or before cadences, and was both prepared for
   and then _____.   [resolved

3. A fifteenth-century Burgundian composer,
   Guillaume Dufay, was among the first to use
   secular tunes in music for the _____.   [Mass

4. The French composer Johannes Ockeghem made
   much use of _____ and its variations.   [canon

5. For his Missa pange lingua, Josquin borrowed
   a phrase from Gregorian chant and used it
   imitatively in each voice of the Kyrie. This
   technique is called the _____ technique.   [paraphrase

6. Amateur music making was encouraged in the
   sixteenth century by a technological advance:
   the art of music _____, which began in 1501.   [printing

7. In the sixteenth century, literary and musical
   trends in Italy created an important new vocal
   composition, the _____.   [madrigal

8. A popular English vocal composition known as
   the _____ was related to the madrigal and   [ballett
   usually had a "fa-la-la" refrain.

9. Renaissance instruments were grouped in families,
   or _____.   [consorts

10. Many instrumental works began as adaptations
    of _____ music.   [vocal

True or False:

11. One of the most important polyphonic techniques
    of the Renaissance was imitation.   [true

36

12. Polyphony remained more important than homophony
    throughout the Renaissance period.   [true

Multiple Choice:

13. The Italian madrigal of the sixteenth century
    helped develop the art of
    a. text painting.
    b. unison singing.
    c. stanzaic form.   [a

14. A Renaissance composer who later wrote some of
    the first operas was
    a. Palestrina.
    b. Monteverdi.
    c. Morley.   [b

15. In sixteenth-century England, the favorite
    household instrument was the
    a. lute.
    b. harpsichord.
    c. piano.   [b

Matching:

16. Ricercar   ____ a stately dance   [19
17. Canzona   ____ originally a chanson   [17
18. Fantasia   for instruments
19. Pavane   ____ an imitative, contra-   [16
20. Galliard   puntal piece patterned
                           on the motet
                      ____ an instrumental work   [18
                           using imitative tech-
                           niques in free style
                      ____ a quick dance in   [20
                           triple meter

DIRECTED LISTENING

Josquin: Kyrie of the Missa pange lingua (Side 2, Band 9)

1. As each voice or part enters, it repeats the
   word "Kyrie"
   a. an octave higher than the last voice.
   b. in melodic imitation.
   c. to a new theme.   [b

2. The meter is
   a. duple.
   b. triple.
   c. a combination of the two.   [b

3. The texture is
   a. polyphonic.
   b. monophonic.
   c. strophic.   [a

4. The listener hears
   a. a constant use of tone painting.
   b. a highly syncopated rhythm.
   c. long, flowing contrapuntal lines.   [c

Palestrina: Kyrie of the <u>Missa brevis</u> (Side 2, Band 10)

1. The Kyrie of the <u>Missa brevis</u> is
   a. accompanied by organ.
   b. accompanied by organ and brass instruments.
   c. sung without accompaniment.   [c

2. Palestrina's polyphonic technique
   a. makes use of imitative phrases in each voice.
   b. is similar to that of Leonin.
   c. in rudimentary, yet still affecting.   [a

3. The Kyrie is essentially
   a. modal and exotic.
   b. chromatic and intensely emotional.
   c. tonal and serene.   [c

4. The voices in the last "Kyrie" section enter
   in which of the following orders?
   a. Bass--tenor--alto--soprano
   b. Tenor--alto--soprano--bass
   c. Alto--tenor--soprano--bass   [b

Monteverdi: "Si ch'io vorrei morire" (Side 2, Band 11)

1. The madrigal is sung with
   a. harpsichord accompaniment.
   b. lute accompaniment.
   c. no accompaniment.   [c

2. To express the drama of the text, Monteverdi
   a. used text painting and dissonance.
   b. allowed one solo voice to narrate the words
      while the rest sing softly in the background.
   c. used instruments to double the voice.   [a

3. During the middle portion, there are long
   sequences during which suspended dissonances
   a. hang unresolved.
   b. are resolved one after the other.
   c. are all resolved to a unison on the tonic.   [b

4. The madrigal begins with a
   a. major triad.
   b. minor triad.
   c. dissonant chord.   [a

Morley: "Now Is the Month of Maying" (Side 2, Band 12)

1. For the most part, the voices move
   a. in a complex contrapuntal texture.
   b. in consecutive, imitative phrases.
   c. together, in a chordal texture.   [c

2. The form is
   a. monophonic.
   b. strophic.
   c. rhapsodic.   [b

3. The refrain is built on the syllables
   a. fa-la-la.
   b. tirra-lirra.
   c. cuck-oo.   [a

4. The music emphasizes the
   a. minor mode.
   b. major mode.
   c. chromatic scale.   [b

Cumulative Review
Medieval and Renaissance

SELF-TEST

Matching:

1. Virelai
2. Ballett
3. Discantus
4. Madrigal
5. Canzona
6. Authentic mode
7. Paraphrase technique
8. Trouvère
9. Melisma
10. Proper

___ Mass text   [10
___ singer of love songs   [8
___ solo song based on   [1
    poetic form
___ elaboration of   [7
    existing melody
___ two-part organum   [3
___ Italian song based   [4
    on poetic form
___ early scale pattern   [6
___ instrumental compo-   [5
    sition
___ florid style   [9
___ song with "fa-la-la"   [2
    refrain

Write M for Medieval and R for Renaissance.

___ 11. A rhythmic device called isorhythm   [M
    became a striking aspect of this music.

___ 12. Composers made very careful use of   [R
    dissonance.

____ 13. Dufay and Josquin were outstanding   [R
         composers in this period.

____ 14. Religious music made use of organum and   [M
         discantus styles.

____ 15. Many love songs had monophonic textures.   [M

____ 16. Imitative devices such as canon were used   [R
         in Masses and motets.

____ 17. Music printing began.   [R

____ 18. Composers used text painting to illustrate [R
         the words of a poem in their vocal music.

____ 19. The ars nova style brought changes in rhythm [M
         and harmony.

____ 20. Four- and five-part textures were common.   [R

DIRECTED LISTENING

1. A two-part texture is used in
   a. Leonin's Viderunt omnes (Side 2, Band 7)
   b. Palestrina's Kyrie of the Missa brevis
      (Side 2, Band 10)   [a

2. Greater use of imitation is present in
   a. Morley's "Now Is the Month of Maying" (Side
      2, Band 12)
   b. Josquin's Kyrie of the Missa pange lingua
      (Side 2, Band 9)   [b

3. The rhythm is freer in which of the following
   pieces?
   a. Monteverdi's "Si ch'io vorrei morire" (Side
      2, Band 11)
   b. Machaut's "Douce dame jolie" (Side 2, Band 8) [a

4. Although both Machaut's "Douce dame jolie" (Side
   2, Band 8) and Ventadorn's "Be m'an perdut" (Side
   2, Band 6) are love songs, they differ in that
   one is
   a. polyphonic and the other is monophonic.
   b. accompanied and one is not.   [b

9

Introduction to Baroque Music

KEY TERMS AND CONCEPTS

Melody and Rhythm
  Stile Rappresentativo and Monody
  Ornamentation
    Trill, Turn, Arpeggio
  Solo Performance and Virtuosity
  Recitative, Aria, Arioso
  Bel Canto Style
  Freer Rhythm in Recitative
Harmony and Texture
  Major-Minor Harmony System
    Chordal Progression
    Modulation
  Equal Temperament
  Greater Use of Dissonance
  Homophonic and Polyphonic Textures
  Basso Continuo
    Figured Bass
Timbre and Dynamics
  Violin Family, Wind Instruments, Organ, Harpsichord
  Beginning of Orchestra
  Terraced Dynamics
Types of Compositions and Form
  Opera, Cantata, Oratorio
  Sonata, Concerto, Fugue, Suite
  Multi-Movement Works
  Ritornello and Fugal Forms
Concertato Style

SELF-TEST

Completion Questions:

1. Through their interest in reviving ancient
   Greek drama, the members of the Camerata
   developed a new musical style known as the
   _____.   [stile rap-
                                                      presentativo

2. The term _____ indicates the use of one   [monody
   principal melody with a simple chordal
   accompaniment.

3. Although early Baroque melodies were fairly
   simple, singers could insert _____ where   [ornamenta-
   appropriate for effective expression.   tion

4. Gradually, the stile rappresentativo
   developed into two main types: the _____   [recitative
   and the aria.

5. Soon after 1630, the reaction against
   excessive ornamentation led to the
   _____ style.   [bel-canto

6. The change from polyphonic to monodic style
   was paralleled by the development of
   _____ harmony.   [major-minor

7. Changes of key, or _____, became a basic   [modulation
   compositional tool during the Baroque period.

8. The basso continuo style provided a _____   [homophonic
   texture typical of much Baroque music.

9. The use of sudden, sharp changes in dynamic
   level is known as _____ dynamics.   [terraced

10. Baroque vocal music was mainly homophonic,
    but in instrumental music _____ remained
    important as well.   [polyphony

Multiple Choice:

11. The Baroque period spans, roughly, the years
    a. 1500-1650.
    b. 1600-1750.
    c. 1618-1648.   [b

12. The earliest stile rappresentativo stressed
    a. a metrical rendering of ancient poetic
       forms.
    b. a musical declamation of the text in
       accordance with the natural rhythm of
       the words.
    c. a new consciousness in which music was to
       be used for the greater glory of God.   [b

13. During the Baroque period, instrumental music
    a. became as important as vocal music.
    b. became much more important than vocal
       music.
    c. was generally based on transcriptions of
       vocal music.   [a

14. In the equal- or well-tempered scale, the
    distance between consecutive notes
    a. becomes smaller as one proceeds up the
       scale.
    b. becomes greater as one proceeds up the
       scale.
    c. is the same in one key as in another.   [c

15. A form of shorthand notation in which the
    melody and the bass line are written out
    while chords are indicated through numbers
    placed over or under the bass line is
    known as
    a. contrabass.
    b. basso profundo.
    c. figured bass.   [c

16. In this system, the accompanist or keyboard
    player is expected to
    a. realize the bass by playing the indicated
       chords.
    b. play the bass line, while the string
       instruments realize the chords.
    c. tell the string players which chords
       to use.   [a

44

17. In the concertato style
    a. one soloist plays with a small chamber
       ensemble.
    b. groups play or sing in alternation with
       each other.
    c. two small ensembles play simultaneously.   [b

Matching:

18. Trill   ____ a group of four or   [19
19. Turn   five notes that
20. Arpeggio   "turn around" the
                        principal note

                   ____ a chord whose notes   [20
                        are played one after
                        the other instead
                        of simultaneously

                   ____ a note played in   [18
                        rapid alternation
                        with the note just
                        above it

DIRECTED LISTENING

1. Monteverdi's "Tu se' morta" (Side 3, Band 5)
   offers an example of
   a. monody.
   b. recitative.
   c. chordal progression.   [a

2. Texture in the first movement of Handel's
   Concerto in B♭ Major (Side 3, Band 3) is
   basically
   a. polyphonic.
   b. homophonic.
   c. monophonic.   [b

3. The texture of the chorus of Handel's "For
   Unto Us a Child Is Born" (Side 3, Band 7)
   is _____ until near the end when it
   becomes _____.
   a. homophonic--polyphonic
   b. polyphonic--homophonic
   c. polyphonic--monophonic   [b

4. The first movement of Vivaldi's Winter Concerto
   (Side 3, Band 2) features a solo instrument
   of the
   a. string family.
   b. woodwind family.
   c. brass family.   [a

5. The "affection" most stimulated in the first
   movement of Bach's Cantata No. 80 (Side 3,
   Band 6) is
   a. fear.
   b. joy.
   c. anger.   [b

IO
Baroque Instrumental Music

KEY TERMS AND CONCEPTS

Development and Standardization of Orchestra
Sonatas
  Trio, Solo, Unaccompanied
  Church and Chamber
  Slow--Fast Pattern
Concertos
  Concerto Grosso
    Concertino and Ripieno
  Solo Concerto
    Soloist and Ripieno
  Contrast and Homophonic Texture
  Ritornello Form
  Fast--Slow--Fast Pattern
Fugue
  Subject and Episodes
  Countersubject
Suite
  Solo and Ensemble
  Dance Movements
    Allemande, Courante, Sarabande, Gigue
Other Types of Compositions
  Sinfonia and Overture (French and Italian)
  Toccata and Fantasia

SELF-TEST

Completion Questions:

1. The country that provided the dominant musical
   ideas during the early Baroque era was _____. [Italy

2. The German composer _____ wrote masterpieces   [J. S. Bach
   in almost all types of Baroque music.

3. Before 1600, composers rarely specified the
   precise _____ for their works. By 1750,   [instrumentation
   at the close of the Baroque, they usually did.

4. By the mid-eighteenth century, the orchestra
   was fairly standardized, consisting usually
   of a basic _____ section plus several   [string
   wind instruments.

5. The _____ sonata for one melody instrument   [solo
   and continuo became popular, because it gave
   the new virtuoso performer a chance to display
   great skill.

6. Baroque characteristics that are important in
   the concerto form include contrast between
   large and small groups, a basically _____   [homophonic
   texture, and the idea of combining several
   short sections in a single composition.

7. A very mature form of imitative counterpoint
   is found in the _____.   [fugue

8. The basis of the fugue is a melody, called
   the main theme or _____, which is stated   [subject
   at the beginning by a single voice, then
   taken up in succession by the other voices.

9. Another compositional form developed during
   the Baroque period, the _____, consists   [suite
   of a number of movements, each like a dance
   and all in the same key or related keys.

10. The _____, a form of prelude, became a   [toccata
    vehicle for keyboard instruments during the
    Baroque period.

48

Multiple Choice:

11. During the seventeenth century, a new form
    emerged from the sinfonia:
    a. the concerto grosso.
    b. the Italian overture.
    c. the suite.   [b

12. In a concerto grosso, the two groups of
    players are known as the
    a. tutti and ripieno.
    b. concertino and ripieno.
    c. ripieno and concertati.   [b

13. The ritornello form--common in concertos--is
    a pattern in which
    a. the first movement is constructed to show
       the musical potential of the solo instrument.
    b. the same opening theme is used as the basis
       for each movement.
    c. the ripieno passages return to the opening
       theme, while the solo passages often change
       it or elaborate on it in virtuoso fashion.   [c

Matching:

14. Domenico Scarlatti   ____ composed a large   [15
15. François Couperin   number of ordres
16. Jean-Baptiste Lully   or suites for
17. Arcangelo Corelli   harpsichord
18. Giuseppe Torelli
19. Girolamo Frescobaldi   ____ gave the French   [16
20. Johann Sebastian   overture its form
    Bach
                                ____ wrote the earliest   [18
                                      solo concerto

                                ____ was the supreme   [20
                                      master of fugue

                                ____ created the concerto   [17
                                      grosso form

                                ____ wrote over six   [14
                                      hundred sonatas for
                                      harpsichord

                                ____ was an early composer [19
                                      of toccatas

DIRECTED LISTENING

Scarlatti: Sonata in C Major, K. 159 (Side 3, Band 1)

1. The character of the opening theme of the sonata is
   a. sustained and solemn.
   b. quick and sprightly.
   c. lyric and exalted.   [b

2. The opening theme begins in C major but quickly brings in frequent F sharps. This suggests that Scarlatti is modulating to the dominant key of
   a. D major.
   b. A major.
   c. G major.   [c

3. The sonata is organized in
   a. one continuous movement.
   b. two sections.
   c. three sections.   [b

4. The rhythmic character of the work is
   a. subtle and underplayed.
   b. highly irregular and complex.
   c. driving and strongly accented.   [c

Vivaldi: Winter Concerto, First Movement (Side 3, Band 2)

1. The repeated notes played by the ripieno at the opening of the movement
   a. form the material that is used in the ritornello.
   b. are heard only here and serve as a brief introduction.
   c. are heard later in the solo part.   [a

2. The repeated notes build into a
   a. consonant chord.
   b. dissonant chord.
   c. modal chord.   [b

3. The solo violin moves mainly in
   a. long, sustained tones.
   b. rapid tones.
   c. an isorhythmic pattern.   [b

4. The overall tonality of the movement is
   a. major.
   b. minor.
   c. modal.   [b

Handel: Concerto in B♭ Major, First Movement
(Side 3, Band 3)

1. The arpeggios of the first theme presented
   by the ripieno outline the notes of the
   a. dominant chord (F major).
   b. tonic chord (B♭ major).
   c. subdominant chord (E♭ major).   [b

2. These arpeggios return
   a. only once again, at the end.
   b. in the second section.
   c. in typical ritornello style.   [c

3. The three instruments in the concertino are
   a. one horn and two violins.
   b. two oboes and one violin.
   c. one flute, one oboe, and one violin.
   d. two violins and one viola.   [b

4. The overall tonal feeling of the work is
   a. major.
   b. minor.
   c. highly dissonant.   [a

Bach: Fugue in G Minor (Side 3, Band 4)

1. Melodic movement at the beginning of the
   subject, or main theme, is
   a. conjunct.
   b. disjunct.   [b

2. The number of voices is
   a. two.
   b. three.
   c. four.
   d. five.   [c

3. The second and later presentations of the
   subject are accompanied by
   a. chordal harmony.
   b. a countersubject.
   c. doubling in the higher ranges.
   d. episodes.   [b

4. During the exposition, or first section,
   a. each voice presents the subject once.
   b. the first voice is dominant throughout.
   c. only the subject is presented.
   d. the first two voices pass the subject
      back and forth between them.   [a

II
Baroque Vocal Music

KEY TERMS AND CONCEPTS

Opera
  Gradual Enrichment of Early Highly Monodic Style
  Types of Recitatives
    Secco and Accompagnato
  Types of Arias
    Strophic-Bass, Ostinato, Da Capo
  Major Styles
    Monteverdi and the Venetian School
    A. Scarlatti and the Neapolitan School
    Lully and the French School
    Purcell and the English School
    Opera Buffa
Cantata
  Italian Secular Cantata
  German Sacred Cantata
Oratorio
Mass
  <u>Missa brevis</u>

SELF-TEST

Completion Questions:

1. The monodic style gave composers a compositional
   method that blended the rhythms, melodies, and
   harmonies of _____ with those of music.   [speech

2. Bel canto composers preferred light, _____   [lyrical
   melodies and smooth rhythms.

3. The vocal style known as recitativo
   _____ was accompanied only by continuo.   [secco

4. The _____ aria, frequently used   [strophic-bass
   during the years before 1630, consisted of
   a number of consecutive stanzas, the melodies
   of which are varied over a repeated bass line.

5. The _____ aria was made up of three sections,   [da capo
   of which the third was a repetition of the
   first, often with improvised embellishments.

6. Italian comic opera, known as opera _____,   [buffa
   appeared soon after 1700.

7. The only country in which a distinctly non-
   Italian style of opera developed was _____.   [France

8. The German sacred cantata resulted from a
   blending of Italian melodic style with older
   _____ vocal types.   [polyphonic

9. Like operas, oratorios consisted of contrasting
   sections of recitative, aria, and chorus. They
   differed from opera principally in making greater
   use of the _____ for narrative and dramatic   [chorus
   purposes.

10. J. S. Bach wrote four works entitled _Missa_ _brevis_
    as well as his great masterpiece, the _Mass_ _in_
    _____, a complete setting of the Ordinary.   [B Minor

Multiple Choice:

11. Neapolitan opera composers
    a. introduced a revitalized polyphonic style.
    b. adopted a homophonic style that subordinated
       the instrumental parts to the vocal.
    c. revived ancient Greek tragedies, setting
       the dialogue to monodic declamation.   [b

12. The French opera style was marked by
    a. shortened **arias**, the inclusion of scenic
       spectacles, and colorful orchestrations.
    b. the lack of an orchestra.
    c. plots of a light and frivolous nature,
       usually satirizing some aspect of contem-
       porary French life.   [a

13. Bach ordinarily ended his cantatas with
    a. an instrumental postlude.
    b. a postlude for organ.
    c. a harmonized chorale.   [c

Matching:

14. Giulio Caccini   ___ created the continuo   [15
15. Claudio Monteverdi   madrigal form and
16. Alessandro Scarlatti   composed Orfeo
17. Jean-Baptiste Lully   ___ a composer of German   [19
18. Henry Purcell   birth who emigrated
19. Georg Friedrich Handel   to England and wrote
20. J. S. Bach   many oratorios
                            ___ wrote cantatas and   [20
                                 Masses that are now
                                 considered the glory
                                 of the Baroque era
                            ___ regarded as the creator [17
                                 of French opera
                            ___ generally considered   [16
                                 the founder of
                                 Neapolitan opera
                            ___ wrote Euridice, the   [14
                                 first surviving opera
                            ___ composed Dido and   [18
                                 Aeneas, an opera
                                 still performed today

DIRECTED LISTENING

Monteverdi: "Tu se' morta" from Orfeo (Side 3, Band 5)

1. In Monteverdi's "Tu se' morta," the
   accompaniment is played by
   a. full orchestra.
   b. organ and lute.
   c. violin and basso continuo.   [b

2. Great use is made of
   a. text painting.
   b. unresolved dissonance.
   c. imitative counterpoint.   [a

3. The mood of the music is one of
   a. hopeless despair.
   b. joy in victory.
   c. despair and growing resolution.   [c

4. The mode is
   a. minor throughout.
   b. minor, changing briefly to major.
   c. mainly major.   [a

Bach: Cantata No. 80, First Movement (Side 3, Band 6)

1. In the opening movement, Bach makes much use of
   a. ornamental embellishments such as turns
      and trills.
   b. text painting.
   c. imitative counterpoint.   [c

2. The first movement is sung
   a. with harpsichord accompaniment.
   b. with orchestral accompaniment.
   c. without accompaniment.   [b

3. The overall feeling of the movement is
   a. meditative.
   b. jubilant.
   c. mournful.   [b

4. The voices are doubled by
   a. violins.
   b. woodwinds.
   c. harpsichord.   [a

56

Handel: "For Unto Us a Child Is Born" from Messiah (Side 3, Band 7)

1. In this work, Handel expresses joy through
   the use of
   a. a major key.
   b. a dominant key.
   c. contrasting major and minor sections.   [a

2. The first two melodic phrases are set in
   a. chorale variation style.
   b. parallel thirds.
   c. contrapuntal imitation.   [c

3. The setting of the words "Wonderful! Counselor!
   the Mighty God, the Everlasting Father, the
   Prince of Peace!" is best described as
   a. chordal.
   b. monodic.
   c. operatic.   [a

4. The setting of the text gives the final words
   a. emphasis and certainty.
   b. greater volume.
   c. enriched tonal color.   [a

Bach: Sanctus of the Mass in B Minor, First Section
(Side 3, Band 8)

1. In the opening section, the word "Sanctus" is
   set with the voices moving primarily in
   a. parallel motion.
   b. contrary motion.
   c. unison.   [a

2. The orchestral accompaniment is
   a. subordinate to the vocal parts.
   b. a full partner in the total contrapuntal
      texture.
   c. reduced to organ and continuo.   [b

3. The rhythmic feeling is
   a. relatively slow, in triple meter.
   b. slow, with beats subdivided into triplets.
   c. moderate, with a gradual accelerando.   [b

4. The texture is
   a. polyphonic with homophonic passages.
   b. strongly contrapuntal.
   c. predominantly homophonic.   [c

57

Cumulative Review
Medieval to Baroque

SELF-TEST

Matching:

1. Recitativo secco
2. Paraphrase technique
3. Monody
4. Tenor
5. Dorian
6. Fantasia
7. Imitative
      counterpoint
8. Isorhythm
9. Rondeau
10. Basso continuo

___ voice singing chant   [4
      melody
___ harmonic support to   [10
      a melody by two
      instruments
___ lightly accompanied   [1
      declamatory style
___ repetition of same   [7
      theme by different
      voices
___ elaboration of   [2
      existing melody
___ Church mode   [5
___ repeated pitch and   [8
      rhythm pattern
___ free instrumental work   [6
___ song based on poetic   [9
      form
___ style stressing melody   [3
      line

Write M for Medieval, R for Renaissance, and B for Baroque

____ 11. The instrumental canzona developed from   [R
a vocal model.

____ 12. Rhythmic complexity was achieved with   [M
isorhythm.

____ 13. The pavane and galliard were popular dances. [R

____ 14. Orchestras were standardized and often   [B
professional.

____ 15. Styles of opera developed in Venice, Naples, [B
and France.

____ 16. Music was notated with neumes.   [M

____ 17. Although harmony was based on modes, com-   [R
posers now used twelve modes instead of eight.

____ 18. Love songs were sung by troubadours and   [M
trouvères in France.

____ 19. Terraced dynamics and imitative counterpoint [B
were techniques used to achieve repetition
and contrast.

____ 20. The madrigal saw its greatest development in   [B
the continuo madrigal and as a chamber vocal
form.

DIRECTED LISTENING

1. A major difference between the first movement
   of Bach's Cantata No. 80 (Side 3, Band 6) and
   Palestrina's Kyrie of the Missa brevis (Side
   2, Band 10) is
   a. lack of accompaniment in one and imitative
      counterpoint in the other.
   b. use of isorhythm in one and paraphrase
      technique in the other.
   c. fugal exposition in one and declamatory
      style in the other.   [a

2. Leonin's <u>Viderunt omnes</u> (Side 2, Band 7) and
   Bach's Sanctus of the <u>Mass in B Minor</u> (Side
   3, Band 8) are similar in their use of
   a. orchestral accompaniment.
   b. melismatic style.
   c. fugue.   [b

3. Which song seems to be based on a dance rhythm?
   a. Ventadorn's "Be m'an perdut" (Side 2, Band 6)
   b. Machaut's "Douce dame jolie" (Side 2, Band 8) [b

4. The entrances of the voices in Handel's "For Unto
   Us a Child Is Born" (Side 3, Band 7) and Josquin's
   Kyrie of the <u>Missa pange lingua</u> (Side 2, Band 9)
   differ in which of the following ways?
   a. They enter on the same note in Handel's work
      but at an interval of a fifth in Josquin's.
   b. Handel's entrance is a fugue while Josquin's
      is homophonic.   [a

12
Introduction to Classical Music

KEY TERMS AND CONCEPTS

Transitional Period
  Rococo Style
  Empfindsamer Stil
Classical-Romantic Continuum
Melody and Rhythm
  New Emphasis on Melody
  Regular Phrase Structure
  Rhythmic Variety
Harmony and Texture
  Major-Minor Harmony and Modulation
    Related Keys
    Relative Majors and Minors
  Homophonic and Polyphonic Textures
Timbre and Dynamics
  Expanded Orchestra
  Pianoforte
Types of Compositions and Form
  Opera, Mass, Oratorio
  Sonata Cycles
    Symphony, Concerto, Sonata, String Quartet
  Sonata Form
    Exposition, Development, Recapitulation
    Introduction and Coda
  Rondo Form

SELF-TEST

Completion Questions:

1. An elaborate, ornamented style of the late
   Baroque period was known as _____.   [Rococo

2. Whereas Baroque instrumental music often had
   many overlapping layers of melody, Classical
   music usually featured _____ melodic line(s), [one
   clearly heard.

3. One of the chief characteristics of the Classical
   style is the organization of music into clearly
   heard, regularly recurring _____.   [phrases

4. The largest portion of a Classical orchestra was
   the _____ section.   [string

5. The Mannheim orchestra was noted for its use of
   great contrast in _____ effects.   [dynamic

6. The modern symphony orchestra is somewhat
   _____ in size than those of Classical times, [larger
   but its balance of instrumentation is fundamentally similar.

7. The _____ gradually replaced the harpsichord [piano
   during the Classical period.

8. In longer compositions of the Classical period,
   modulation from the tonic to the _____ key   [dominant
   became common practice.

9. There are several forms of the minor mode, all of
   which differ from the major in that the _____ [third
   tone is lowered a half step.

10. The alteration of a theme by changes in such ele-
    ments as rhythm, timbre, dynamics, and harmony,
    or by expanding or contracting it, is known as
    _____.   [development

True or False:

11. By the middle of the eighteenth century, the
    Baroque style had begun to decline in
    popularity.   [true

12. The Empfindsamer Stil rejected the basic
    proposition that music could, in any way,
    convey emotion.   [false

13. The music of the Classical period is generally
    characterized by steady meter.   [true

14. During the Classical period, the theme of a
    composition was rarely varied or developed
    in any way.   [false

Multiple Choice:

15. The regular phrases of Classical music tend
    to give the music a
    a. stress on variety.
    b. sense of proportion.
    c. lighter texture than was common during
       the Baroque era.   [b

16. In the Classical style, the rhythm of the
    melody is often variable. The rhythm of the
    accompaniment tends to be
    a. much more regular.
    b. even less regular.
    c. similar to that of the melody.   [a

17. The major key most closely related to the
    key of C major would be
    a. D major.
    b. G major.
    c. A major.   [b

18. A common practice during the Classical period
    was to open a composition in a minor key and
    then modulate to the
    a. dominant.
    b. subdominant.
    c. relative major.   [c

19. A sonata cycle is a
    a. structured form that includes an exposition, development, and recapitulation.
    b. sequence of three or four movements, each cast in a specific form.
    c. group of sonatas written by one composer, usually in the same or related keys.   [b

20. Sonata form, sometimes called sonata-allegro form, includes the following three sections:
    a. exposition, development, and recapitulation.
    b. theme, variation, and theme restatement.
    c. statement of the subject, episode, and fugal development.   [a

---

DIRECTED LISTENING

1. The first movement of Mozart's Symphony No. 40 in G Minor (Side 4, Band 3) achieves dramatic changes in mood through
   a. abrupt changes in dynamics and rhythm.
   b. sudden transitions to polyphonic texture.   [a

2. The form of the third movement of Beethoven's Piano Sonata in C Minor, Op. 13 (Side 6, Band 2) is
   a. theme and variations.
   b. rondo.
   c. sonata.   [b

3. The melodic motion at the beginning of the opening theme of the first movement of Beethoven's String Quartet No. 7 in F Major (Side 6, Band 3) is
   a. ascending.
   b. descending.
   c. static.   [a

4. Haydn achieves dramatic changes in mood in the first movement of the Symphony No. 94 in G Major (Side 4, Band 1) by
   a. abrupt changes in tempo and polyphonic interplay.
   b. striking changes in instrumentation.   [a

5. The dominant orchestral section in the first
   movement of Mozart's Piano Concerto No. 17 in
   G Major (Side 6, Band 1) is made up of
   a. keyboard and percussion instruments.
   b. strings.
   c. woodwinds.   [b

13

The Classical Symphony: Haydn and Mozart

KEY TERMS AND CONCEPTS

Symphony
  Basic Structure
    Four Movements
    Fast--Slow--Moderate--Fast Pattern
  General Use of Form
    First Movement in Sonata Form
    Second Movement in Binary, Sonata, or Theme and Variations Form
    Third Movement in Ternary Form (Minuet and Trio)
    Fourth Movement in Sonata, Rondo, or Sonata-Rondo Form
  Concept of Dramatic Development from Within

SELF-TEST

Completion Questions:

1. Franz Josef Haydn was the first important master
   of the sonata for orchestra, a work more often
   called the _____.   [symphony

2. Although the position of hired musicians in the
   eighteenth century was not prestigious, there
   were many advantages to the _____ system.   [patronage

3. Haydn's music draws on the _____ songs of   [folk
   his native Austria.

4. The height of Haydn's symphonic art is apparent in the series of symphonies commissioned in 1791 by Johann Peter Salomon, the _____ Symphonies. [London

5. First performed in London in 1792, Haydn's Symphony No. 94 in G Major quickly became known as the "_____" Symphony. [Surprise

6. The second movement of Haydn's Symphony No. 94 is marked andante, or walking tempo, and is in _____ form. [theme and variations

7. The fourth movement of the same symphony has characteristics of both sonata and _____ forms. [rondo

8. Although Mozart remained always firmly rooted in Classical tradition, his later work shows the beginning of a pull toward the _____ style. [Romantic

9. Today, each of Mozart's compositions bears a _____ number. [Köchel

10. The first movement of Mozart's Symphony No. 40 in G Minor begins with a _____-note motive that suggests the drama of the entire symphony. [three

Multiple Choice:

11. Many of Haydn's early symphonies are
    a. quite short and light.
    b. surprisingly dissonant and dramatic.
    c. simply folk dances for orchestra. [a

12. Haydn was one of the first composers to
    a. develop themes in the Classical way.
    b. write in so many forms.
    c. compose love songs to his patrons' wives. [a

13. The surprise in Haydn's Symphony No. 94 in G Major is achieved through a sudden sharp change in
    a. harmony.
    b. tempo.
    c. dynamic level. [c

14. The characteristic meter of the minuet is
    a. duple.
    b. triple.
    c. either of the above at the composer's
       discretion.   [b

15. The patronage system proved
    a. as helpful to Mozart as to Haydn.
    b. to be Mozart's salvation.
    c. unbearable to Mozart.   [c

16. Symphony No. 40 is among Mozart's
    a. earliest symphonies.
    b. middle symphonies.
    c. last symphonies.   [c

Match the symphonic movements with the forms most
typically used.

17. First movement   ___ sonata, rondo, or   [20
18. Second movement   sonata-rondo
19. Third movement   ___ binary, sonata, or   [18
20. Fourth movement   theme and variations
                          ___ sonata   [17
                          ___ ternary   [19

DIRECTED LISTENING

Haydn: Symphony No. 94 in G Major, First Movement
(Side 4, Band 1)

  1. The first movement opens with a
     a. peaceful introduction.
     b. short overture.
     c. rousing statement of the main theme.   [a

  2. The first theme is introduced by the
     a. cellos.
     b. violins.
     c. flutes.   [b

3. The development section of the first movement
   uses motives from the themes along with
   a. scales, arpeggios, and repeated notes.
   b. long sequences of trills.
   c. a new theme.   [a

4. The texture of the first movement is generally
   a. monodic.
   b. polyphonic.
   c. homophonic.   [c

Haydn: Symphony No. 94 in G Major, Second Movement
(Side 4, Band 2)

1. The theme of the second movement includes
   prominent
   a. conjunct motion.
   b. parallel motion.
   c. thirds.   [c

2. The theme is played first by the
   a. violins.
   b. cellos.
   c. oboes.   [a

3. To achieve the surprise, the orchestra suddenly
   a. plays much more softly.
   b. plays much more loudly.
   c. stops completely.   [b

4. The movement ends
   a. with a crashing finale.
   b. softly.
   c. with a full fugue on the theme.   [b

Mozart: Symphony No. 40 in G Minor, First Movement
(Side 4, Band 3)

1. The three-note motive is played first by
   a. the cellos.
   b. the violins.
   c. one oboe.   [b

2. The rhythm of the opening three-note motive might
   best be described as
   a. long--short--long.
   b. short--long--short.
   c. short--short--long.   [c

3. The second theme descends in
   a. conjunct fashion.
   b. disjunct fashion.
   c. thirds.   [a

4. A powerful unifying force in the first movement
   is provided by the
   a. rondo structure.
   b. theme and variations structure.
   c. repetitive rhythm of the opening motive.   [c

Mozart: Symphony No. 40 in G Minor, Third Movement
(Side 4, Band 4)

1. The meter of this movement is basically
   a. duple.
   b. triple.
   c. irregular.   [b

2. The minuet theme is
   a. triadic and clearly tonal.
   b. chromatic and winding.
   c. built on an ascending scale.   [a

3. The rhythmic pulse of the minuet theme
   contains an element of
   a. staccato.
   b. suspense.
   c. syncopation.   [c

4. Texture is thinnest in the
   a. first minuet section.
   b. trio.
   c. second minuet section.   [b

70

14

The Classical Symphony: Beethoven

KEY TERMS AND CONCEPTS

Late Classical Developments in the Symphony
  Expansion of Classical Forms
    Coda as Second Development Section
  Programmatic Aspects
  Single Motivic Idea in Successive Movements
  Scherzo for Third Movement

SELF-TEST

Completion Questions:

1. Beethoven believed in _____ as the mark   [originality
   of the artist.

2. Beethoven was the first musician of common
   background to mix with the _____ on his   [aristocracy
   own terms.

3. Beethoven _____ Classical forms instead   [expanded
   of discarding them.

4. Beethoven's Symphony No. 6, the _____,   ["Pastoral"
   draws on the imagery of the countryside.

5. Symphony No. 3, the "Eroica," was originally
   conceived as a tribute to _____.   [Napoleon

6. The opening _____-note motive of Symphony   [four
   No. 5 is one of the most famous in all symphonic
   literature.

7. The motive conveys what Beethoven sensed as the
   remorseless energy of _____.   [fate

8. This motive is stated, restated, and infinitely
   changed; it appears in other movements as well,
   helping to create a new _____ in the symphony. [unity

9. The third movement of Symphony No. 5 is often
   called a _____, or "joke."   [scherzo

10. After Symphony No. 5, Beethoven wrote only
    _____ more symphonies.   [four

True of False:

11. Beethoven was grateful for the lessons he
    received from Haydn and said often that his
    music owed much to the rules of composition
    taught him by the older Classical master.   [false

12. While never subservient, Beethoven realized
    that by accepting the Classical tradition
    as it stood he would ensure his art a loyal
    patronage.   [false

13. During Beethoven's lifetime, the fabric of
    monarchic and aristocratic European society
    was torn by revolution and chaos.   [true

Multiple Choice:

14. In 1792 Beethoven left Bonn to study in
    a. Vienna.
    b. Berlin.
    c. Italy.   [a

15. Which of the following was **not** characteristic
    of Beethoven's musical style?
    a. Rejection of all traditional rules
    b. Addition of new elements of timbre
    c. A lengthening of the coda section   [a

16. Not until Beethoven
    a. were musicians allowed to read their parts
       from scores rather than commit them to memory.
    b. did a single motivic idea reappear in each
       movement of a symphony.
    c. did most political leaders realize the power-
       ful influence music could wield.   [b

17. Symphony No. 5 was profoundly influenced by
    Beethoven's
    a. revolutionary ardor.
    b. sensitive love of the countryside.
    c. struggle with despair over his deafness.   [c

18. The most important relationship to be found in
    the opening motive of Symphony No. 5 is the
    a. melodic one.
    b. harmonic one.
    c. rhythmic one.   [c

19. Which description applies to the scherzo form?
    a. Normally in duple meter
    b. Usually in ternary or ABA form
    c. Generally played only by the woodwind instru-
       ments of the orchestra   [b

20. Symphony No. 9 differs from Beethoven's other
    symphonies in that it was written
    a. in one long, continuous movement.
    b. as a dirge to be played at his own funeral.
    c. for orchestra, choir, and vocal soloists.   [c

DIRECTED LISTENING

Beethoven: Symphony No. 5 in C Minor, First Movement
(Side 5, Band 1)

1. The rhythm of the opening motive is
   a. long--short--long--short.
   b. short--long--short--long.
   c. short--short--short--long.   [c

2. Beethoven varied the motive by
   a. changing the tonal pattern.
   b. changing the rhythmic pattern.
   c. both of the above.   [a

3. The fanfare introduction to the second theme
   is played by the
   a. trumpets.
   b. trombones.
   c. horns.   [c

4. The first movement ends with
   a. the recapitulation.
   b. the development.
   c. a coda in which the first theme is further
      developed.   [c

Beethoven: Symphony No. 5 in C Minor, Second
Movement (Side 5, Band 2)

1. The second movement contrasts with the first
   in its
   a. tempo and key.
   b. orchestral texture.
   c. highly contrapuntal style.   [a

2. Within the movement there are
   a. one theme and seven variations.
   b. two important themes.
   c. three important themes.   [b

3. The first theme is introduced by the
   a. first violins.
   b. cellos and violas.
   c. woodwinds.   [b

4. The meter of the movement is
   a. duple.
   b. triple.
   c. changing.   [b

Beethoven: Symphony No. 5 in C Minor, Third
Movement (Side 5, Band 3)

1. The third movement is in
   a. sonata form.
   b. rondo form.
   c. ternary form.   [c

2. The second theme consists of
   a. a dancelike country tune.
   b. the familiar rhythmic motive used on a
      single repeating tone.
   c. rapid scale passages.   [b

3. The theme in Section B is introduced by
   a. flutes and clarinets.
   b. trumpets and trombones.
   c. cellos and double basses.   [c

4. The first section of the movement then
   returns, but is played
   a. more softly.
   b. more forcefully.
   c. in fugal treatment.   [a

Beethoven: Symphony No. 5 in C Minor, Fourth
Movement (Side 5, Band 3--Immediately following
Third Movement)

1. The movement is in
   a. ritornello form.
   b. rondo form.
   c. sonata form.   [c

2. The opening is dominated by the majestic
   sound of the
   a. strings.
   b. brass.
   c. woodwinds.   [b

3. During the development there is a
   a. return of the original motive and parts
      of the preceding movement.
   b. complete repetition of the themes brought
      out in the exposition.
   c. choral rendering of Schiller's "Ode to Joy."   [a

4. The symphony ends
   a. in a presto rush toward conclusion.
   b. with a long, brooding restatement of the
      original motive.
   c. with material from the second movement.   [a

15
The Classical Concerto

KEY TERMS AND CONCEPTS

Classical Concerto
  Soloist and Orchestra
  Basic Structure
    Three Movements
    Fast--Slow--Fast Pattern
  General Use of Form
    First Movement in Sonata Form with Double Exposition
    Second Movement Varies
    Third Movement in Rondo or Theme and Variations Form
  Cadenza Passages for Virtuosic Display

SELF-TEST

Completion Questions:

1. The solo concerto of the Classical period
   developed from the _____ concerto.   [Baroque

2. The dramatic function of the solo part in a
   concerto is similar to that of the _____   [aria
   in an opera.

3. Although the functions of orchestra and soloist in a concerto are different, the two are of _____ musical importance.

    [equal

4. During certain passages, generally toward the end of a movement, the orchestra remains silent while the soloist plays a spontaneous-sounding, usually rapid and difficult passage called a _____.

    [cadenza

5. The Classical concerto almost always consists of _____ movements.

    [three

6. The _____ ordinarily announces the first theme, and sometimes others as well.

    [orchestra

7. The _____ movement that appears in the Classical symphony is usually omitted in the Classical concerto.

    [minuet

8. Other Classical composers, including _____ and his brother, Michael, wrote important concertos for a variety of instruments.

    [Haydn

9. Beethoven's concertos and symphonies clearly illustrate the _____ continuum.

    [Classical-Romantic

10. Beethoven's most important concertos are five for _____ and one for violin.

    [piano

True or False:

11. A concerto involves a musical confrontation between a solo instrument and the orchestra.

    [true

12. Classical concertos occasionally featured more than one solo instrument.

    [true

13. Baroque composers such as Torelli and Vivaldi wrote solo violin concertos as vehicles to display their own virtuosity.

    [true

14. The emergence of instrumental homophony in the Classical period favored the supremacy of a melody instrument.

    [true

Multiple Choice:

15. The Classical concerto is basically a
    a. symphony.
    b. sonata cycle.
    c. instrumental oratorio.   [b

16. The most common tempo pattern in the Classical
    concerto is
    a. fast--slow--fast.
    b. slow--fast--slow.
    c. fast--moderate--slow.   [a

17. The form of the first movement is modified
    to include
    a. two expositions.
    b. two developments.
    c. one exposition and two developments.   [a

18. In comparison with the modern piano, that of
    Mozart's time had a
    a. greater dynamic capacity and more sonorous
       tone.
    b. very similar dynamic capacity.
    c. limited dynamic capacity and a finer, more
       crystalline tone.   [c

19. A coda is a
    a. concluding section.
    b. small interlude between the music of the
       soloist and the entrance of the orchestra.
    c. composition for solo instrument and small
       ensemble.   [a

20. Beethoven refashioned the Classical concerto
    in a
    a. new two-movement form.
    b. richer, more contrapuntal style.
    c. more expressive, dramatic, and Romantic
       style.   [c

DIRECTED LISTENING

Mozart: Piano Concerto No. 17 in G Major, First
Movement (Side 6, Band 1)

1. The concerto is opened by the
   a. full orchestra.
   b. piano.
   c. piano and orchestra together.   [a

2. The first orchestral theme is given to the
   a. cellos.
   b. first violins.
   c. oboes.   [b

3. After the orchestral exposition, the piano
   soloist plays the first theme in
   a. exact repetition of the orchestra.
   b. a shortened version.
   c. a more elaborate version.   [c

4. After the repetition of the second theme,
   the piano
   a. gives way once more to the orchestra.
   b. begins a new and playful "piano theme"
      of its own.
   c. plays the third theme of the orchestral
      exposition in alternation with the orchestra.   [b

16
Classical Chamber Music:
The Sonata
and the String Quartet

KEY TERMS AND CONCEPTS

Chamber Music
  One Player per Part
    Instrumental Dialogue
    Clear and Transparent Texture
  One or Two Players for Sonatas
  Small Ensembles for String Trios, String Quartets, Piano
    Quartets, etc.
Sonata
  Three to Four Movements
  Predominantly for Piano
String Quartet
  Four Movements
  First Violin, Second Violin, Viola, Cello

SELF-TEST

Completion Questions:

1. Chamber music is usually defined as music
   composed for a small group of performers,
   with only _____ player(s) for each part.   [one

2. Most Classical sonatas were written for
   _____.   [piano

3. The first movement of a Classical sonata is typically in _____ form.   [sonata

4. Beethoven's Piano Sonata in C Minor, Op. 13 is often called the _____.   ["Pathétique"

5. The most important type of Classical string ensemble was the _____, which took definite form under Haydn.   [string quartet

6. At first, the lower strings in the string quartet were limited to _____, in deference to the Classical preference for homophony.   [accompaniment

7. Early string quartets were kept simple, since they were written mainly to be performed by _____ musicians.   [amateur

8. Many early string quartets, including some by Haydn, were called _____, music for entertainment.   [divertimenti

9. Each of Beethoven's three Razumovsky quartets is considerably _____ than quartets by either Haydn or Mozart.   [longer

10. Quartet No. 7, the first of the Razumovsky series, is in four movements, each organized in _____ form or a modification of it.   [sonata

True or False:

11. The conductor of the string quartet assumed a new and special importance.   [false

12. The string quartet usually consisted of first violin, second violin, viola, and cello.   [true

13. Generally, in chamber music, there are two players for each part.   [false

14. Beethoven tended to use the quartet as a medium for experimentation.   [true

Multiple Choice:

15. The chamber work achieves its effect by
    setting up between the instruments
    a. a feeling of competitive tension.
    b. a system in which two instruments play
       in unison while the other two explore
       the melody.
    c. an ever-changing dialogue.   [c

16. A bridge between Classical and Romantic styles
    can be seen in the piano sonatas of Beethoven
    and
    a. Schubert.
    b. Haydn.
    c. C. P. E. Bach.   [a

17. In early string quartets, the melody was
    almost invariably given to the
    a. viola.
    b. cello.
    c. violin.   [c

18. Haydn allowed the lower voices of the string
    quartet to become
    a. more independent.
    b. louder in relation to the top two voices.
    c. solo instruments within the ensemble.   [a

19. Although the separate voices of the quartet
    were given greater independence, the basic
    texture was still essentially
    a. monophonic.
    b. polyphonic.
    c. homophonic.   [c

20. Mozart's popular serenade Eine kleine Nacht-
    musik ("A Little Night Music") is usually
    played by
    a. a string quartet.
    b. thirteen wind instruments.
    c. a small chamber orchestra.   [c

DIRECTED LISTENING

Beethoven: Piano Sonata in C Minor, Op. 13, Third
Movement (Side 6, Band 2)

1. How many distinct themes occur in the movement?
   a. Five
   b. Four
   c. Three   [c

2. The meter of the first theme is
   a. duple.
   b. triple.
   c. irregular.   [a

3. The first theme recurs
   a. twice.
   b. three times.
   c. four times.   [c

4. The piece gradually diminishes in intensity
   and then
   a. fades out.
   b. ends with a fast and brilliant scale passage.
   c. ends with quiet chords.   [b

Beethoven: String Quartet No. 7 in F Major,
First Movement (Side 6, Band 3)

1. The opening theme is played by the
   a. violin.
   b. viola.
   c. cello.   [c

2. The melodic motives of the movement are given
   a. mostly to the cello.
   b. mostly to the violins.
   c. to all of the instruments more or less
      equally.   [c

3. One of the ways in which Beethoven provides
   accompaniment for the instrument that happens
   to have the melody is to write
   a. an optional piano part.
   b. a series of soft, repetitive notes for the
      three remaining instruments.
   c. an optional basso continuo to be used at the
      performers' discretion.   [b

4. The texture of the movement shifts easily from
   a. polyphonic to homophonic.
   b. monophonic to homophonic.
   c. monophonic to polyphonic.   [a

17
Classical Vocal Music

KEY TERMS AND CONCEPTS

Nature of Opera
  Conventional Limitations
  Expressive Advantages
Materials of Opera
  Solo Voices
  Arias and Recitatives
  Choruses and Ensembles
  Orchestra
    Accompaniment
    Overtures and Interludes
  Libretto and Synopsis
  Scenery and Staging
Classical Opera Styles
  Opera Seria
  Opera Buffa
  Singspiel
Classical Oratorios and Masses
  Incorporation of Symphonic Characteristics

SELF-TEST

Completion Questions:

1. Opera, like any form of art, has certain
   _____ that must be accepted if we are to   [conventions
   enjoy it.

2. In opera, where the most important element is
   music, plot and character are often condensed
   and _____.   [stylized

3. The _____ is the highest of the usual male   [tenor
   voices, and is frequently used for the protag-
   onist's or lover's part.

4. The text or script for the opera is called
   the _____.   [libretto

5. The orchestra generally opens an opera with
   an _____.   [overture

6. Opera _____ is fast-paced and humorous,   [buffa
   full of frivolity, practical jokes, and
   comic confusion.

7. In another comic form, the German _____,   [Singspiel
   the recitative is replaced by spoken dialogue.

8. The librettist for The Marriage of Figaro
   was _____, a theater poet at the   [Lorenzo
   court of Emperor Joseph II in Vienna.   da Ponte

9. Beethoven composed a variety of vocal works,
   including two Masses, an oratorio, and a choral
   fantasia for piano, chorus, and orchestra. The
   Missa _____ in D major is considered one of   [solemnis
   his greatest achievements.

10. In Beethoven's Masses, the individual sections
    begin to resemble the _____ of a symphony.   [movements

Multiple Choice:

11. Classical composers of vocal music used
    the forms developed in the
    a. Middle Ages.
    b. Renaissance.
    c. Baroque period.   [c

12. Opera is best described as a combination of
    a. vocal and instrumental music.
    b. music for soloists and ensemble.
    c. music and theater.   [c

13. The highest and most virtuosic of the
    soprano voices is the
    a. lyric.
    b. dramatic.
    c. coloratura.   [c

14. During the Classical period, the leading
    masters of opera composition were generally
    a. Italian-speaking.
    b. French-speaking.
    c. German-speaking.   [c

15. As the Classical movement took hold, reformers
    tried to make the opera seria
    a. shorter and more dramatic.
    b. less serious.
    c. simpler and more emotionally direct.   [c

16. The Abduction from the Seraglio and
    The Magic Flute are Mozart's two
    a. opera seria.
    b. opera buffa.
    c. Singspiel.   [c

Matching:

17. Franz Josef Haydn   ____ Idomeneo   [19
18. Pierre-Augustin   ____ Fidelio   [20
    de Beaumarchais   ____ The Creation   [17
19. Wolfgang Amadeus   ____ La Folle journée   [18
    Mozart
20. Ludwig van
    Beethoven

88

Directed Listening

Mozart: "Cinque, dieci" from <u>The Marriage of Figaro</u> (Side 6, Band 4)

1. Figaro's rhythmic theme is anticipated by the
   a. violins.
   b. oboes.
   c. cellos.   [a

2. Susanna's lyrical theme is anticipated by the
   a. violins.
   b. oboes and clarinets.
   c. cellos.   [b

3. Which of the following techniques is used at
   the words "Ah, il mattino alle nozze vicino"?
   a. Imitation
   b. Text painting
   c. Two-part harmony in parallel motion   [c

4. During the repetition of "Ora si ch'io
   son contenta" by both Figaro and Susanna,
   Mozart makes use of
   a. modulation.
   b. imitation.
   c. strong dissonance.   [b

Cumulative Review
Medieval to Classical

SELF-TEST

Matching:

1. Basso continuo
2. Coda
3. Concerto grosso
4. Opera buffa
5. Caccia
6. Madrigal
7. Chanson
8. Sonata cycle
9. Tempus perfectum
10. Camerata

___ comic vocal work [4

___ five-part song using [6
    text painting

___ harpsichord and [1
    cello part

___ extended ending [2

___ early French [7
    secular song

___ orchestral piece with [3
    two opposing sections

___ Florentine group of [10
    poets and musicians

___ overall form of [8
    symphony

___ triple meter [9

___ imitative Italian song [5

Write M for Medieval, R for Renaissance,
B for Baroque, and C for Classical.

___ 11. A basso continuo was a standard [B
    instrumental accompaniment.

____ 12. Composers began to set the texts of secular   [M
         songs over Latin texts in polyphonic vocal
         works.

____ 13. The coda was expanded into a second area of   [C
         melodic development.

____ 14. Discantus style became more popular than   [M
         organum style.

____ 15. Opera developed out of Italian interest in   [B
         the classics.

____ 16. Poetic forms, such as the rondeau, were   [M
         set as secular songs.

____ 17. The harpsichord was a popular instrument.   [B

____ 18. The piano concerto usually had a double   [C
         exposition.

____ 19. Both tempus perfectum and tempus imperfectum   [M
         began to be considered acceptable meters.

____ 20. The fugue was a common contrapuntal   [B
         composition for keyboard instruments.

DIRECTED LISTENING

1. A major difference between the opening of
   Vivaldi's Winter Concerto, Op. 8, No. 4, in
   F Minor (Side 3, Band 2) and the opening of
   Mozart's Piano Concerto No. 17 in G Major
   (Side 6, Band 1) is the
   a. lack of orchestral introduction in the
      Winter Concerto.
   b. presence of a double exposition in the
      Piano Concerto.
   c. tempo marking.   [b

2. Scarlatti's Sonata in C Major (Side 3, Band 1)
   and the third movement of Beethoven's Piano
   Sonata No. 13 in C Minor (Side 6, Band 2) share
   which of the following characteristics?
   a. Use of both major and minor modes
   b. Unchanging dynamic level
   c. Binary form   [a

3. The first movements of Handel's Concerto in
   Bb Major, Op. 3, No. 1 (Side 3, Band 3) and
   Beethoven's String Quartet No. 7 in F Major
   (Side 6, Band 3) both use a group of solo
   instruments with equal melodic roles.
   Beethoven's work differs from Handel's, however,
   in that it does not
   a. have basso continuo support.
   b. use violins.
   c. have more than one theme.   [a

4. Which piece makes the greatest use of imitative
   counterpoint?
   a. Bach's Fugue in G Minor (Side 3, Band 4)
   b. The first movement of Vivaldi's Winter
      Concerto (Side 3, Band 2)   [a

18
Introduction to Romantic Music

KEY TERMS AND CONCEPTS

Romantic Characteristics
  Individualism
    Artist as Hero and Rebel
  Nature, the Exotic, the Supernatural
  Interaction of All the Arts
Melody and Rhythm
  Lyricism
  Rhythmic Experimentation
Harmony and Texture
  Harmonic Experimentation
    Modulation, Chromaticism, Dissonance
  Textural Variety and Complexity
Timbre and Dynamics
  Larger Orchestra
  Greater Dynamic Range
Types of Compositions and Form
  Short Compositions
    Piano Pieces and Lieder
  Long Compositions
    Sonata Cycles
  Program Music
    Program Symphonies, Symphonic Poems, Overtures,
      and Incidental Music
  Choral Music and Opera
  Use of Classical Forms

Completion Questions:

1. Romantic art was much _____ subjective   [more
   than Classical art.

2. In painting, the interest in experiment led
   to the revival of earlier styles, notably
   the _____ style.   [Gothic

3. The English poet _____ exemplified the   [Byron
   wittier side of Romanticism in his Don Juan.

4. Whereas Classical melody used small motives,
   logically developed, Romantic melody was
   more _____ in character.   [lyrical

5. In comparison with Baroque and Classical
   rhythms, Romantic rhythm is more _____   [varied
   and complex.

6. Romantic composers made much use of the
   tension created by harmonic conflict,
   or _____.   [dissonance

7. They also employed a great deal of _____ --   [chromaticism
   that is, the use of tones that are not part of
   the key in which a work is written.

8. Romantic textures could be more complicated
   and _____ than in earlier times, partly   [denser
   because orchestras were now larger than before.

9. German art songs of the Romantic period were
   called _____.   [Lieder

10. Music that is related to extramusical
    elements such as a story or a picture
    is known as _____ music.   [program

True or False:

11. Romantic artists, musicians, and poets were
    great innovators and rejected totally the works
    of art done by their predecessors in earlier
    times.   [false

12. Romantic composers emphasized melody even more
    than their predecessors.   [true

13. Romantic composers rejected all use of
    counterpoint.   [false

14. The sonata cycle remained the basis for the
    symphony, string quartet, concerto, and
    sonata in the Romantic era.   [true

Multiple Choice:

15. Which of the following did not influence the
    growth of the Romantic movement?
    a. The social and political upheavals of the
       preceding era
    b. A widespread desire to change the world
       for the better
    c. A general curiosity about the exotic, occult,
       and supernatural
    d. A lessening of patriotic zeal
    e. An admiration for the workings of the
       imagination   [d

16. Which of the following was not characteristic
    of the standard Romantic hero?
    a. Melancholy
    b. Optimism
    c. A fascination with death and the supernatural
    d. A keen understanding of beauty and pain   [b

17. The decline of the patronage system gave artists
    a new freedom to
    a. innovate and infuse their art with the
       passion of their own inner lives.
    b. use their art to rally support against the
       state.
    c. use their art to glorify God and the Church.
    d. use their art to imitate the scientific
       exactitude required in the machine age.   [a

18. Which of the following would be an especially
    likely subject for a Romantic painting?
    a. Aristocrats gathered in a drawing room
    b. A group of steelworkers in a factory
    c. A still life of a bowl of fruit
    d. Peasants working in the fields   [d

19. Which of the following was the primary
    Romantic poet in Germany?
    a. Baudelaire
    b. Keats
    c. Nietzsche
    d. Goethe   [d

20. Music meant to be performed during the course
    of a play or other entertainment is known as
    a. interlude music.
    b. incidental music.
    c. symphonic breaks.
    d. program music.   [b

DIRECTED LISTENING

1. The melodic interval heard at the beginning
   of Chopin's Nocturne in E♭ Major, Op. 9, No. 2
   (Side 7, Band 1) is
   a. ascending.
   b. descending.
   c. static.   [a

2. Which two elements contribute most to the mood
   of sadness and despair in Schubert's "Gute
   Nacht" (Side 7, Band 3)?
   a. Tempo and timbre
   b. Mode and melodic direction
   c. Texture and instrumentation   [b

3. The sense of passion in Schumann's "Widmung"
   (Side 7, Band 4) is largely reflected by the
   a. piano part and the dramatic change in
      dynamics.
   b. mode and tempo of the melody.
   c. singer's contemplative interpretation.   [a

4. Romantic composers often idealized the adventures of heroes. In Strauss's tone poem <u>Till Eulenspiegels lustige Streiche</u> (Side 8, Band 2), the hero Till is musically portrayed as a
   a. dispairing lost soul.
   b. mischievous rogue.
   c. gallant knight.   [b

5. The form of Liszt's <u>Hungarian Rhapsody No. 6 in D♭ Major</u> (Side 7, Band 2) is
   a. ternary.
   b. sonata.
   c. ABCD.   [c

19

Romantic Piano Music

KEY TERMS AND CONCEPTS

Romantic Piano Style
  Lyrical and Dramatic Emphasis
  Frequent Programmatic Associations
  Stylistic Innovations
    Legato and Rubato
Continued Composition of Sonatas
New "Character" Pieces
  Nocturnes
  Études and Preludes
  Dances
    Mazurkas, Polonaises, Waltzes
  Ballades and Scherzos
  Rhapsodies

SELF-TEST

Completion Questions:

1. Whereas Classical works for solo piano had
   been largely _____, Romantic   [sonatas
   composers developed a number of different
   types of compositions.

2. The composer who perhaps did the most to establish the piano as a voice of Romanticism was _____.

[Frédéric Chopin

3. Chopin's melodies are characteristically written in a smooth _____ style.

[legato

4. Chopin also utilized a technique in which very small displacements in rhythm are introduced for expressive purposes. This is called _____.

[rubato

5. Chopin extracted the _____ movement from the sonata cycle and treated it as a work in itself.

[scherzo

6. Chopin's Polish heritage was particularly apparent in his use of the _____ forms of his homeland.

[dance

7. The great violin virtuoso _____ was an important influence on Liszt's piano style.

[Niccolò Paganini

8. Liszt was encouraged to experiment with piano timbre by his practice of transcribing _____ compositions for piano.

[orchestral

9. Among Liszt's most successful piano works were his heroic _____.

[rhapsodies

10. An important series of rhapsodies are Liszt's fifteen _____ Rhapsodies.

[Hungarian

Multiple Choice:

11. Which of the following composers wrote almost exclusively for the piano?
   a. Liszt
   b. Schubert
   c. Schumann
   d. Chopin

[d

12. In Paris in the nineteenth century, the
    pianist was
    a. considered unimportant.
    b. the star of the salon.
    c. often featured as an entertainer in
       fashionable restaurants.
    d. secondary in popular appeal only to the
       solo violinist.   [b

13. In Chopin's piano compositions, intensity is
    usually achieved by
    a. repeating the melody and accompaniment with
       such variations as increased ornamentation,
       dynamic change, rubato, and syncopation.
    b. developing the theme.
    c. improvisations on the theme.   [a

14. Which of the following wrote music that was
    the most technically difficult to play?
    a. Liszt
    b. Chopin
    c. Schumann
    d. Beethoven   [a

Matching:

15. Ballade   ____ a work intended to   [17
16. Polonaise   express the mood of
17. Nocturne   night
18. Étude   ____ an exercise to develop   [18
19. Rhapsody   piano technique
20. Mazurka   ____ a narrative piece for   [15
                              piano
                         ____ a heroic dance of   [16
                              ceremonial importance
                         ____ a Slavic dance in $\frac{3}{4}$ [20
                              meter with Eastern
                              European rhythms
                         ____ a freely structured   [19
                              work, dramatic or he-
                              roic in tone, rich in
                              emotional color,
                              scored to achieve a
                              large sound, and com-
                              monly written for
                              piano or orchestra

100

DIRECTED LISTENING

Chopin: Nocturne in E♭ Major, Op. 9, No. 2
(Side 7, Band 1)

1. The first time the main theme occurs, it is
   accompanied by
   a. fluid chords that sound on every beat.
   b. dense, sustained chords.
   c. rippling arpeggios.   [a

2. The main theme is immediately
   a. followed by a secondary theme.
   b. repeated the same way.
   c. repeated with ornamentation.   [c

3. Throughout the piece, the main theme under-
   goes
   a. progressive ornamentation.
   b. extreme variation until it is completely
      obscured.
   c. identical repetition.   [a

4. The third and last theme functions as a
   a. recapitulation.
   b. transition to the return of the first theme.
   c. coda.   [c

Liszt: Hungarian Rhapsody No. 6 in D♭ Major
(Side 7, Band 2)

1. The rhythm of the first section is
   a. steady and marchlike.
   b. uneven, with constant rubato.
   c. pulsing and dancelike.   [b

2. In the second section, the melody is
   a. conjunct and lyrical.
   b. motivic and disjunct.
   c. heavily syncopated.   [c

3. The mode in the third section is
   a. major.
   b. minor.
   c. not clearly defined.   [b

4. The fourth section begins with simple
   melody that is
   a. repeated once.
   b. followed by three other new melodies.
   c. repeated four times with increasing
      complexity.   [c

20
Romantic Song

KEY TERMS AND CONCEPTS

Development of the Lied
  Related Events
    Improvements in the Piano
    Wealth of German Poetry
  Characteristics
    Compound Art Form (Literature and Music)
    Piano-Voice Partnership
  Structure
    Generally Free or Modified Strophic
    Other Forms
  Use of Symbolism
    Imitation of Nature
    Narrative and Emotional Expression
French Art Song
  Lighter and Less Introspective

SELF-TEST

Completion Questions:

1. The earliest development of the Romantic art
   song took place in the _____-speaking   [German
   countries.

2. A song in which each stanza is set to the same melody is said to be in _____ form.   [strophic

3. A major factor in the popularity of Lieder was the continued improvement of the _____.   [piano

4. Composition of Lieder was further encouraged by the writing of a great deal of _____ in Germany at about this time.   [poetry

5. In Lieder, the piano part is usually _____ from the melody.   [different

6. In "Gute Nacht," Schubert used a _____ _____ form.   [modified strophic

7. Schumann combined his career as a composer with that of a music _____, in which role he was successful and influential.   [critic

8. A younger German composer who greatly admired Robert and Clara Schumann and became a major composer of Lieder and other works was

   _____.   [Johannes Brahms

9. In Mahler's Lieder, the singer was often accompanied not by piano but by _____.   [orchestra

10. Another country where the art song was important in this period was _____.   [France

Multiple Choice:

11. When several art songs are composed around a central poetic theme or story, the group is called
    a. an opera.
    b. a Lieder.
    c. a song cycle.
    d. an oratorio.   [c

12. Which of the following did **not** influence the
    growth of Lieder in the nineteenth century?
    a. The continued improvement of the piano
    b. The Romantic artists' search for freer forms
       in which to express their feelings
    c. A decrease in new opera works that freed
       singers to perform other types of music
    d. The writing of lyric poetry   [c

13. In a typical Lied, the piano part
    a. occasionally duplicates the vocal melody line.
    b. never duplicates the vocal melody line.
    c. always duplicates the vocal melody line.
    d. generally repeats the vocal melody line.   [a

14. Schubert wrote
    a. many songs, but almost no other music.
    b. three superb song cycles, and a small
       amount of instrumental music.
    c. several hundred songs and numerous instru-
       mental works.
    d. many solo songs and a number of magnificent
       choral works.   [c

15. Which composer's works are thought to mark the
    culmination of the German Romantic Lied?
    a. Schubert
    b. Wolf
    c. Mahler
    d. Strauss   [b

16. Whereas German Lieder tend to be intensely
    introspective and profound, French art songs
    of the late nineteenth century are generally
    a. lighter and more elegant.
    b. introspective to the point of madness.
    c. satiric.
    d. sensitive and serious.   [a

Matching:

17. Schubert   ____ Four Serious Songs   [20
18. Schumann   ____ Leider eines   [19
19. Mahler   fahrenden Gesellen
20. Brahms   ____ Dichterliebe   [18
                     ____ Erlkönig   [17

105

DIRECTED LISTENING

Schubert: "Gute Nacht" from Die Winterreise
(Side 7, Band 3)

1. The lover's trudging through the snow is
   suggested by the
   a. percussive melody line.
   b. motivic accompaniment.
   c. duple meter and repeated chords.   [c

2. "Gute Nacht"
   a. never moves out of the minor mode.
   b. never moves out of the major mode.
   c. alternates between major and minor modes
      in a varying pattern.   [c

3. Which of the following does Schubert use as
   an expressive device in "Gute Nacht"?
   a. Changing accompaniment with each new stanza
   b. Repetition of certain lines of the text in a
      kind of refrain
   c. The sound of a babbling brook   [b

4. The melody in "Gute Nacht"
   a. is exactly the same in each stanza.
   b. changes somewhat in each stanza.
   c. remains the same in the verse, but varies in
      the chorus section of the song.   [b

Schumann: "Widmung" (Side 7, Band 4)

1. The meter is
   a. duple.
   b. triple.
   c. unsteady because of rubato.   [b

2. The song opens with a
   a. sustained chord followed by the melody in
      the right hand.
   b. rushing piano arpeggio.
   c. long trill dissolving into a cadenza-like
      passage.   [b

3. Section B is announced by a
   a. vocal cadenza.
   b. syncopated figure in the left hand.
   c. key change and disappearance of the
      piano arpeggios.   [c

4. The piece ends with
   a. staccato chords.
   b. a sustained chord that fades out.
   c. a rushing piano arpeggio.   [c

21
Romantic Symphony and Concerto

KEY TERMS AND CONCEPTS

Types of Symphonies
  Program and Abstract
Characteristics of the Abstract Symphony
  Lyricism and Rhythmic Variety
  Harmonic Experimentation
    Chromaticism
    Remote Key Relationships
    Chords with Added Tones
  Dense Texture
  Contrasts in Timbre and in Melody
  Free Use of Classical Forms
Romantic Concerto
  Emphasis on Virtuosity
  Freer Interplay Between Soloist and Orchestra

SELF-TEST

Completion Questions:

1. The roots of the Romantic symphony are found
   in the works of Beethoven and _____.   [Schubert

2. Liszt and Berlioz contributed heavily to the development of the _____ symphony, a composition that derives its logic and form from a literary or artistic work.

[program

3. Other composers, including Mendelssohn, Schumann, and Brahms, wrote _____ symphonies that retained the purely musical organization of the Classical symphony.

[abstract

4. Romantic symphonies emphasized the repetition and variation of lyrical melodies, in contrast to Classical symphonies, which emphasized the logical development of shorter _____.

[motives

5. Chromaticism was _____ common than in the past.

[more

6. Symphonies became denser and more complex in _____ as the orchestra grew in size.

[texture

7. Both Schubert and Beethoven wrote symphonies of _____ rather than four movements.

[five

8. Tchaikovsky wrote several scores for _____, including Swan Lake and The Nutcracker Suite.

[ballet

9. With his predilection for melody, it is not surprising that Tchaikovsky's symphonies are strongly _____.

[lyrical

10. Romantic individualism greatly affected the concerto, creating increased emphasis on _____ elements in the solo part.

[virtuoso

Multiple Choice:

11. Brahms' early compositions were greatly influenced by the works of
    a. Tchaikovsky and Scriabin.
    b. Schubert and Schumann.
    c. Strauss and Mahler.
    d. Chopin and Liszt.

[b

12. Bach, Beethoven, and Brahms represent the masters of which three periods of music?
    a. Renaissance, Baroque, and Romantic
    b. Baroque, Romantic, and Post-Romantic
    c. Baroque, Classical, and Romantic
    d. Classical, Romantic, and Impressionist   [c

13. Tchaikovsky is particularly admired for his
    a. melodies.
    b. integration of chorus with orchestra in his symphonies.
    c. imaginative use of dissonance and unresolved chords.
    d. chromaticism.   [a

14. Which two symphonies open with a "fate" motive?
    a. Brahms' Symphony No. 3 and Mendelssohn's "Reformation" Symphony
    b. Beethoven's Symphony No. 5 and Tchaikovsky's Symphony No. 4.
    c. Tchaikovsky's Symphony No. 6 and Beethoven's Symphony No. 5.
    d. Franck's Symphony in D Minor and Tchaikovsky's Symphony No. 4.   [b

15. Which of the following are noted for the large scale of their orchestral compositions?
    a. Beethoven and Tchaikovsky
    b. Franck and Dvořák
    c. Bruckner and Mahler
    d. Schubert and Schumann   [c

16. Which of the following was an occasional Romantic departure from the Classical concerto format?
    a. An equal part for the orchestra, with no virtuoso effects
    b. Bringing in the soloist at once without an orchestral exposition
    c. Using a chamber orchestra to accompany the soloist
    d. The use of the trumpet as the solo instrument   [b

Matching:

17. Tchaikovsky
18. Franck
19. Brahms
20. Mendelssohn

___ "Reformation" Sym- [20
___   phony
___ 1812 Overture [17
___ Symphony in D Minor [18
___ Variations on a Theme [19
___   by Haydn

DIRECTED LISTENING

Brahms: Symphony No. 3 in F Major, First Movement
(Side 7, Band 5)

1. The movement opens with two sustained chords
   played by
   a. woodwinds and brass.
   b. brass and strings.
   c. woodwinds and strings.
   d. brass alone. [a

2. The main theme is introduced in the third
   measure by the
   a. woodwinds.
   b. trumpets.
   c. cellos.
   d. violins. [d

3. The second theme contrasts with the first by
   a. the addition of previously unused
      instruments.
   b. a tempo change.
   c. a change in key, rhythm, and texture. [c

4. The coda is based on
   a. a motive that dissolves into the second
      theme.
   b. entirely new material.
   c. a motive drawn from the first theme. [c

111

Tchaikovsky: Violin Concerto in D Major, Third
Movement (Side 8, Band 1)

1. The orchestral opening is followed by
   a. the main theme played by the solo violin.
   b. a brief violin cadenza.
   c. the main theme played by the strings.   [b

2. The second theme is introduced by the
   a. strings.
   b. full orchestra.
   c. solo violin in the lower register.   [c

3. The motivic, minor third theme is presented by
   a. solo violin.
   b. solo oboe and clarinet.
   c. solo trumpet.
   d. solo bassoon.   [b

4. The mode of the movement is
   a. predominantly major with one minor theme.
   b. minor except at the very end.
   c. always minor.   [a

22
Romantic Program Music

SELF-TEST

Completion Questions:

1. Music that is purely instrumental and associated
   with nonmusical ideas, often described in a
   program given to listeners, is called _____ [program
   music.

2. Most types of program music make use of
   _____ structure.   [Classical

3. The one important new type of composition
   was the _____.   [symphonic
                                                           poem

4. The two most successful Romantic composers
   of program symphonies were _____ and   [Liszt
   Berlioz.

5. An important musical device in Berlioz'
   Symphonie fantastique is the _____,   [idée fixe
   or recurrent musical theme representing the
   beloved.

6. The symphonic poem, which soon became popular
   with composers, was essentially a program
   symphony in _____ movement(s).   [one

7. Strauss used the Classical form of the _____   [rondo
   for Till Eulenspiegel, finding it well suited
   to the humorous story.

8. Musically, there are more similarities than
   differences between the overture and the
   _____.   [symphonic
                                                           poem

9. Music to introduce and accompany theater works
   is called _____ music because it is inciden-   [incidental
   tal to the action of the drama.

10. In concert performances today, incidental music
    is often performed as a _____ for orchestra.   [suite

Multiple Choice:

11. Most Romantic composers
    a. kept themselves isolated and lived hermit-
       like existences.
    b. died young because of poverty, bad living
       conditions, and malnutrition.
    c. were in close touch with painters, poets,
       actors, and dramatists.   [c

12. Which of the following was never given a
    programmatic slant during the Romantic era?
    a. Concerto
    b. Symphony
    c. Short piano works   [a

13. Which of the following affected Berlioz'
    later conception of music?
    a. His early association of music with church
       and local festivals
    b. His early piano training
    c. His experience of patronage   [a

14. The symphonic poems Orpheus, Mazeppa, Hamlet,
    and The Battle of the Huns were all composed by
    a. Richard Strauss.
    b. Franz Liszt.
    c. Felix Mendelssohn.   [b

Match the musical works with their sources of
inspiration:

15. 1812 Overture   ___ a real or fancied   [17
16. Harold in Italy   experience of the
17. Symphonie   composer
    fantastique   ___ a historical event   [15
18. Pictures at an   ___ a poem   [16
    Exhibition   ___ the plot or mood of a [20
19. Till Eulenspiegels   dramatic work
    lustige Streiche   ___ folk tales   [19
20. Romeo and Juliet   ___ a painting or   [18
                             paintings

DIRECTED LISTENING

Strauss: Till Eulenspiegels lustige Streiche
(Side 8, Band 2)

1. In both of the Till motives heard at the beginning of the piece, Till's wily nature is
   suggested by
   a. chromatic intervals.
   b. wide intervals.
   c. embellishments.
   d. sudden changes in tempo.   [a

115

2. The first escapade is signaled by a cymbal
   crash and
   a. a trumpet arpeggio.
   b. loud bass pizzicatos.
   c. a harp cadenza.
   d. a rapidly rising scale in the clarinets.   [d

3. Till is depicted as a lover by a theme, played
   by the violins, that is based on
   a. the original horn motive.
   b. the original string motive.
   c. new material.   [a

4. The work ends brightly with
   a. new material.
   b. a return to the first two motives.
   c. a transformation of the priest theme.   [b

23
Romantic Opera and Choral Music

KEY TERMS AND CONCEPTS

French Opera
  Grand Opera
  Opéra Comique
  Lyric Opera
Italian Opera
  Increasing Nationalism
  Verismo Movement
German Opera
  Ideological Content
  Wagner's Leitmotivs
Choral Music
  Use of Chorus in Symphonies
  Masses Performed in Concert
  Other Works
    Short Secular Choral Pieces
    Hymns and Oratorios

SELF-TEST

Completion Questions:

1. Two important precursors of Romantic Opera are
   <u>Don Giovanni</u> by Mozart and _____ by   [<u>Fidelio</u>
   Beethoven.

2. A mid-nineteenth-century French opera style that was a compromise between grand opera and opéra comique was _____ opera.   [lyric

3. Bizet's Carmen illustrates the interest in _____ subjects that was widespread in France at the time.   [foreign

4. Il Barbiere di Siviglia is perhaps the best-known work of _____.   [Rossini

5. The major operas of Verdi's middle period are in the tradition of _____ opera, but they are more direct and profound.   [grand

6. Verdi's opera _____ is based on an Alexandre Dumas story about a dying courtesan.   [La Traviata

7. Der Freischütz was an early Romantic opera masterpiece by _____.   [Weber

8. According to Wagner's theories, the musical responsibility in the combined music-drama should rest more with the _____ and less with the vocal soloists than in the past.   [orchestra

9. The use of _____, or recurring motives to depict characters and important ideas, becomes important in Wagner's Lohengrin.   [Leitmotivs

10. Large Romantic choral works were usually either settings of the Mass or _____.   [oratorios

True or False:

11. In early nineteenth-century Italian opera, music was strongly dominant over drama.   [true

12. Choral music was not as vital an aspect of nineteenth-century musical expression as in previous eras.   [true

118

Multiple Choice:

13. Mozart's <u>Don Giovanni</u> influenced composers of
    Romantic operas by its
    a. emphasis on supernatural effects and on
       conflict of principles.
    b. carefree, satirical spirit.
    c. Renaissance subject matter.
    d. use of an expanded orchestra.   [a

14. Which of the following is <u>not</u> characteristic
    of grand opera?
    a. Production on a huge scale
    b. Subject matter based on current national
       developments
    c. Mythological settings
    d. Arias and ensembles connected by recitatives
       rather than spoken dialogue   [c

15. Which of the following represents a peak of
    opera composition in France?
    a. <u>Mignon</u>
    b. <u>William Tell</u>
    c. <u>Otello</u>
    d. <u>Carmen</u>   [d

16. Verdi and Wagner were similar in that both
    a. were deeply influenced by the operas of
       Mussorgsky.
    b. composed predominantly in a lighter vein.
    c. used opera to further their political ideas.
    d. went unappreciated in their own time.   [c

17. Verdi's <u>Otello</u> had the same rejuvenating effect
    on opera seria that his <u>Falstaff</u> had on
    a. Italian lyric opera.
    b. French grand opera.
    c. Italian opera buffa.
    d. English opera.   [c

18. The operas of Mascagni, Leoncavallo, and
    Puccini are similar in that they
    a. generally deal with mythological subjects.
    b. attempt to treat everyday people and events
       in a realistic manner.
    c. often deal with fanciful, lighthearted
       subjects.
    d. are always set in Italy.   [b

19. Wagner perceived himself as a
    a. composer of opera only.
    b. musician par excellence, called to compose
       both operatic and symphonic music.
    c. composer of limited musical talent but
       great dramatic gifts.
    d. music dramatist with a historic destiny to
       fulfill.   [d

20. Which of the following was not characteristic
    of Wagner's most mature works?
    a. Chromaticism
    b. The use of heroic-Teutonic myths
    c. A clear distinction between recitatives
       and arias
    d. The use of a large orchestra   [c

DIRECTED LISTENING

Verdi: "Ah, fors' è lui" and "Sempre libera" from
La Traviata (Side 8, Band 3)

1. The first theme of the first section is
   a. lyrical and major.
   b. lyrical and minor.
   c. halting and major.
   d. halting and minor.   [d

2. The second theme of the first section is
   a. lyrical and major.
   b. lyrical and minor.
   c. halting and major.
   d. halting and minor.   [a

3. The second theme is followed by
   a. a recitative passage leading directly into
      the second section.
   b. a recitative passage ending with an elaborate
      cadenza.
   c. a short harmonic transition into the second
      section.   [b

4. At points of climax in the vocal line of the second section, the singer
   a. slows the tempo freely for expressive purposes.
   b. quickens the tempo to express urgency.
   c. maintains a steady tempo but crescendos.
   d. slows the tempo and diminuendos to a whisper.   [a

Wagner: "Der Ritt der Walküren" from Die Walküre
(Side 9, Band 1)

1. The Valkyrie Leitmotiv is sung by
   a. male bass voices.
   b. female voices.
   c. mixed chorus of males and females.   [b

2. The theme also appears in the
   a. brass.
   b. oboes, clarinets, and bassoons.
   c. xylophone.
   d. strings.   [a

3. The meter is
   a. duple.
   b. triple.
   c. constantly alternating between duple and triple.
   d. free.   [b

4. A repeated octave figure is played by
   a. the cellos.
   b. the low brass.
   c. the upper-register winds and strings.
   d. the basses and low brass.   [c

Wagner: Prelude to Tristan und Isolde
(Side 9, Band 2)

1. The Prelude is most distinguished by its
   a. clearly divided themes.
   b. lyrical melodies.
   c. chromaticism.
   d. tempo contrasts.   [c

2. The Prelude is built on
   a. theme and variations.
   b. short motives.
   c. sonata-allegro form.
   d. dance rhythms.   [b

3. Harmonically, the Prelude
   a. remains in the major mode.
   b. remains in the minor mode.
   c. remains in one key.
   d. moves freely from one key to another.   [d

4. Dynamically, the Prelude
   a. crescendos gradually until it reaches a
      peak and then gradually diminishes.
   b. fluctuates frequently between fortissimo
      and pianissimo.
   c. changes very little.
   d. remains piano throughout.   [a

24
Nationalism, Late Romanticism, and Impressionism

KEY TERMS AND CONCEPTS

Nationalistic Music
  Combination of Classical and Folk Traditions
  Characteristics
    Folk Melodies
    Unusual Rhythms
    New Harmonic Practices
Late Romanticism
  Expanded Use of Chromaticism
  Enlarged Orchestra
  Longer Works
Impressionism
  Freer Melody and Rhythm
  Harmonic Innovations
    Gliding Chords
    Increased Dissonance
    Whole-Tone Scale
  Emphasis on Individual Timbres
  Freer Forms

SELF-TEST

Completion Questions:

1. The strongly nationalistic musical rivalries
   of the nineteenth century ran parallel to the
   _____ struggles of the same period.   [political

2. One of the techniques that Romantic composers
   learned from folk melodies was the use of
   unusual _____ .   [intervals

3. Composers were also attracted by the powerful
   rhythmic _____ of much folk music, especially   [energy
   dance music.

4. One of Mussorgsky's aims was an accurate
   rendering of human _____ in music.   [speech

5. Among late Romantic composers, the basic
   Romantic tendencies were intensified and
   exaggerated. In particular, the use of
   _____ in harmony was extensively developed.   [chromaticism

6. Nine symphonies, scored for huge orchestras
   and sometimes chorus and soloists, were written
   by late Romantic composer _____ .   [Gustav Mahler

7. The term "Impressionism" was first applied in
   derision to the work of a group of avant-garde
   _____ .   [painters

8. The creator and most significant representative
   of Impressionism in music was _____ .   [Claude
                                                          Debussy

9. A chord repeated up and down the staff in
   parallel motion, called a _____ chord, was   [gliding
   a favorite Impressionist device.

10. Debussy used a considerable variety of scales
    in his music, including the _____   [whole-tone
    scale, which divided the octave into six
    equal intervals.

124

Multiple Choice:

11. The Russian Five were united mainly by
    a. opposition to Western idioms.
    b. a common style based on Russian folk music.
    c. a fascination with the Oriental side of
       the Russian heritage.
    d. common training under Anton Rubinstein.   [a

12. Which of the following was not a characteristic
    of late Romantic music?
    a. Use of large orchestras
    b. Innovative harmony, often chromatic
    c. Understatement of rhythm and melody
    d. Lengthening of traditional compositions
       such as the sonata and the symphony   [c

13. Impressionist music sought principally to
    a. appeal to the senses.
    b. appeal to the intellect.
    c. express well-defined emotions.
    d. depict visual images.   [a

14. Which of the following is not a trait of
    Impressionist music?
    a. Suggestive titles
    b. Colorful and changing timbres
    c. Motivic melodies
    d. Major-minor harmonies   [d

Matching:

15. Peer Gynt Suites   ___ Russian   [20
16. Iberia   ___ Bohemian   [19
17. Fantasia on   ___ Spanish   [16
       Greensleeves   ___ English   [17
18. Kullervo   ___ Norwegian   [15
19. The Bartered Bride   ___ Finnish   [18
20. Pictures at an
       Exhibition

125

DIRECTED LISTENING

Mussorgsky: "Promenade" and "Gnomus" from
Pictures at an Exhibition (Side 9, Band 3)

1. The mode of the "Promenade" is predominantly
   a. major.
   b. minor.
   c. alternating between major and minor.   [a

2. The "Promendade" opens with the main theme
   played by solo trumpet followed by
   a. brass choir.
   b. trumpet choir.
   c. a counter-theme in the bass.
   d. a soft echo in the strings.   [a

3. The opening motive of "Gnomus" is played by
   a. low woodwinds.
   b. cellos and basses.
   c. trombones and tubas.   [b

4. "Gnomus" features abrupt changes in
   a. texture.
   b. mood.
   c. dynamics.   [c

Debussy: Prélude à l'après-midi d'un faune
(Side 9, Band 4)

1. The opening theme is introduced by solo
   a. piccolo.
   b. oboe.
   c. clarinet.
   d. flute.   [d

2. A prominent characteristic of the work is
   a. rapid passages in the trumpets.
   b. runs in the harp.
   c. elaborate piano figurations.   [b

3. The dynamics of the piece change
   a. abruptly.
   b. seldom.
   c. gradually.   [c

4. The solo passages throughout the work are
   played predominantly by the
   a. woodwinds.
   b. strings.
   c. woodwinds and brasses.
   d. piano.   [a

Cumulative Review
Medieval to Romantic

SELF-TEST

Matching:

1. Gliding chord
2. Trouvere
3. Sackbut
4. Lied
5. Pentatonic scale
6. Cantata
7. Polyphonic Mass
8. Grand opera
9. Verismo
10. Minuet and trio

___ five-note pattern used [5
    in Chinese music and
    in the music of
    Debussy
___ langue d'oïl [2
___ harmonic progression [1
    in stepwise, parallel
    motion
___ consort instrument [3
___ multi-part liturgical [7
    setting
___ art song [4
___ third movement [10
___ realism in music [9
___ extravagant production [8
___ German sacred work [6

Write M for Medieval, R for Renaissance, B for
Baroque, C for Classical, and Rom for Romantic.

___ 11. Folk tunes and new scales were incorporated [Rom
     into operatic and symphonic works.

____ 12. Many composers favored the massive sound   [Rom
of a large orchestra.

____ 13. A tenor line was used to supply a melody,   [M
and a second upper voice was used to
elaborate upon it.

____ 14. Settings of the Mass would often borrow a   [R
theme from a popular song.

____ 15. The violin, which was developed at this   [B
time, was especially suited to the spirit
of the age.

____ 16. The emphasis shifted from four- and five-   [B
part polyphonic works to a style in which
one solo voice was contrasted with ensemble
passages.

____ 17. Composers began to favor the piano over   [C
the harpsichord.

____ 18. Although earlier forms were used, composers   [Rom
were more interested in lyrical content
and timbre than in thematic development.

____ 19. Chromatic harmony was frequently used in   [Rom
works that were often quite lengthy.

____ 20. A significant development was that duple   [M
meter became as acceptable as triple meter.

DIRECTED LISTENING

1. Tchaikovsky's treatment of the solo instrument
in his Violin Concerto in D Major (Side 8,
Band 1) differs from Mozart's in his Piano
Concerto No. 17 in G Major (Side 6, Band 1)
in that
   a. there is greater symmetry between the
   soloist's part and the orchestra's in
   Mozart's work.
   b. there is greater virtuosic display in
   Mozart's work.
   c. only Tchaikovsky places large orchestral
   passages between cadenzas.   [a

2. Two late nineteenth-century works, Debussy's
   Prélude à l'après-midi d'un faune (Side 9,
   Band 4) and Wagner's Prelude to Tristan und
   Isolde (Side 9, Band 2), differ in which of
   the following ways?
   a. Only Wagner develops themes from short,
      chromatic motives.
   b. Only Debussy used wind instruments to
      present the main thematic material.
   c. Only Wagner's work rejects the Romantic
      tradition.   [b

3. Schumann's "Widmung" (Side 7, Band 4) and
   Machaut's "Douce dame jolie" (Side 2, Band 8)
   are both love songs. Which of the following
   elements is present in Schumann's song but
   not in Machaut's?
   a. Allegro tempo
   b. Expressive accompaniment by a single
      instrument
   c. Love text   [b

4. Mussorgsky's Pictures at an Exhibition as
   orchestrated by Ravel (Side 9, Band 3) and
   Strauss's Till Eulenspiegels lustige Streiche
   (Side 8, Band 2) both achieve a large part
   of their impact through
   a. the prominent use of brass instruments.
   b. repetition of a single theme.
   c. the use of the minor mode.   [a

130

25
Introduction to Early Twentieth-Century Music

KEY TERMS AND CONCEPTS

Major Trends
  Objectivism and Abstraction
  Interest in "Primitive" Sources
  New Nationalism
  Futurism and Microtonal Composition
  Gebrauchsmusik (Functional Music)
  Light and Satirical Styles
  Music Inspired by the Machine Age
  Jazz, Folk, and Popular Music
  Neoclassicism
  Atonality and Serialism
Melody and Rhythm
  Melodic Variety
  Rhythmic Departures
    Ostinato
    Frequent Changes in Meter
Harmony and Texture
  Pandiatonicism
  Bitonality and Polytonality
  Bimodality
  Mixture of Textures
  Renewed Interest in Counterpoint
Timbre and Dynamics
  Emphasis on Percussive Sounds
Types of Compositions and Form
  Some Use of Traditional Patterns
  Wide Experimentation

Completion Questions:

1. The twentieth century gave birth to a number of new artistic movements, including _____,   [Cubism which is generally considered to have begun with the painting of Picasso's Les Demoiselles d'Avignon.

2. In the early twentieth century, there was a growing interest in music from "_____"   [primitive sources, perhaps because it seemed associated with a free and spontaneous way of life.

3. The idea that motion in the visual arts and noise in music were the true aesthetic objects of modern art was proclaimed by the _____.   [Futurists

4. A musical style indigenous to the United States that had an increasing influence on the music of European composers in the early twentieth century is _____.   [jazz

5. In the harmonic style known as _____,   [atonality the composer avoids referring to or creating any specific tonal center in a work.

6. One of the most widely explored elements in early twentieth-century music was _____.   [rhythm

7. A short, repeated pattern called a rhythmic _____ was sometimes used as a means of   [ostinato unifying music.

8. Another technique, called _____, involves   [bimodality the superimposition of the major and minor modes.

9. Increased interest in rhythm led composers to stress _____ timbres in place of the string   [percussive and wind sounds of the nineteenth century.

10. Form was a problem for early twentieth-century composers, because the forms developed in the Classical period depended heavily on the _____ system.   [major-minor

Multiple Choice:

11. Modern dance was the creation of such
    choreographers as
    a. Martha Graham.
    b. Sergei Diaghilev.
    c. Luigi Russolo.   [a

12. World War I was an important artistic
    watershed because
    a. it created a new sense of internationalism
       among Western peoples.
    b. it replaced prewar optimism with a sense of
       disillusionment and hopelessness.
    c. it destroyed many irreplaceable artistic
       and musical documents of the past.   [b

13. Which of the following was not an important
    trend in early twentieth-century music?
    a. Interest in "primitive" musical sources
    b. Neoclassicism
    c. Increase in the size of the orchestra   [c

14. Many early twentieth-century composers looked
    for sources of imagery in
    a. nature.
    b. machines.
    c. history.   [b

15. A light, satiric style was associated with
    a. Erik Satie.
    b. Paul Hindemith.
    c. Anton von Webern.   [a

16. Serialism was an outgrowth of
    a. atonality.
    b. bimodality.
    c. Neoclassicism.   [a

Matching:

17. Paul Hindemith   ___ serialism   [18
18. Arnold Schoenberg   ___ Futurism   [20
19. Igor Stravinsky   ___ Gebrauchsmusik   [17
20. Edgard Varèse   ___ Neoclassicism   [17 and 19

133

DIRECTED LISTENING

1. The second movement of Bartók's <u>Music for
   Strings, Percussion, and Celesta</u> (Side 10,
   Band 1) is striking in its
   a. unusual timbres and electronic sounds.
   b. syncopated rhythm and changes in meter.
   c. use of folk melody.   [b

2. The melody in the "Danse sacrale" from
   Stravinsky's <u>The Rite of Spring</u> (Side 10,
   Band 3) may be best described as
   a. percussive.
   b. atonal.
   c. polytonal.   [a

3. "Mondestrunken," the first movement of
   Schoenberg's <u>Pierrot lunaire</u> (Side 10, Band 4),
   seems most radical in its
   a. use of unusual instruments.
   b. apparent lack of dynamic changes.
   c. spoken melodic line.   [c

4. The texture of much of the development section
   in the first movement of Hindemith's <u>Mathis
   der Maler Symphony</u> (Side 10, Band 2) is
   a. chordal.
   b. contrapuntal.
   c. monophonic.   [b

5. In Webern's <u>Symphony, Op. 21</u> (Side 11, Band 1),
   each instrument frequently plays
   a. only one or two notes before another
      instrument takes over.
   b. long solo passages of virtuosic character.
   c. in closely blended harmony with the other
      instruments in its family.   [a

134

26
New Styles of Tonality

NEW TERMS AND CONCEPTS

Music Based on Some Concept of Tonality
Experiments with Different Musical Elements
  Melody
    Folk and Pre-Romantic Sources
    Octave Displacement
    Motivic Melodies
  Rhythm
    Tendency Toward Strong Rhythms
    Asymmetrical and Changing Meters
    Polyrhythms
    Rhythmic Ostinato and Syncopation
    Rhythmic Transposition of Motives
  Harmony
    Variety of Scales
    Ambiguous Tonality
    Pandiatonicism
    Tone Clusters
    Polyharmony and Polychords
    Uncommon Intervals
  Texture
    New Interest in Counterpoint
    Sparse and Dense Extremes
    Spatial Relationship of Instruments
  Timbre
    Stress on Percussive Sounds
  Form
    Traditional and Innovative
    Forms Based on Motivic Development and Evolution

SELF-TEST

Completion Questions:

1. Of the two main lines of development in twentieth-century music, the more easily compre-
   hensible for most people is that which has
   kept some connection with _____.   [tonality

2. Many of Bartók's works have an _____ quality,   [Oriental
   because they draw on the melodies of Eastern
   European, Arabian, and Turkish folk songs.

3. A melodic device Bartók often used and
   apparently learned from peasant music was
   octave _____.   [displacement

4. For his rhythmic counterpoint, Bartók employed
   several different rhythms simultaneously, a
   device known as _____.   [polyrhythm

5. Hindemith felt that art could not be of lasting
   value unless the artist made a serious effort
   to _____ with the audience.   [communicate

6. Hindemith objected strongly to the constant
   quest for new _____ on the part of fellow   [harmonies
   composers, believing that the number of
   possibilities in this area is naturally
   limited.

7. Hindemith frequently employed a counterpoint
   of chord against chord, called _____.   [polyharmony

8. Among Stravinsky's early compositions were
   several _____ commissioned by Sergei   [ballets
   Diaghilev.

9. In The Rite of Spring, probably the most
   startling innovations involve the element
   of _____.   [rhythm

10. Stravinsky's Neoclassical phase began with his
    orchestration of some eighteenth-century music
    by Pergolesi for a ballet called _____.   [Pulcinella

136

Multiple Choice:

11. Bartók, Hindemith, and Stravinsky represent
    a line of modern musical development that
    attempted to
    a. return to the harmonic style of the
       Baroque and Classical periods.
    b. free itself from all limitations
       of tonality.
    c. recover some of the discipline and refine-
       ment of pre-Romantic music.
    d. set up a single, unified system of composi-
       tion to take advantage of modern technical
       developments.   [c

12. The tonal character of Bartók's harmony is
    a. frequently ambiguous.
    b. always clear.
    c. usually based on the traditional major-minor
       modes.
    d. usually based on pentatonic or modal scales.   [a

13. In texture, Bartók laid particular emphasis on
    a. monophony.
    b. triadic chords.
    c. a richly supported homophony.
    d. counterpoint.   [d

14. Bartók's principles of form and structure are
    fundamentally those of
    a. Classical music.
    b. Baroque music.
    c. Debussy and the Impressionists.
    d. the serialists.   [a

15. The term "music for use" refers to
    a. Futurism.
    b. the doctrine that form follows function.
    c. Gebrauchsmusik.
    d. Klangfarbenmelodie.   [c

16. Hindemith's treatment of melody and rhythm
    is rooted in his training in
    a. medieval German, Renaissance, and Baroque
       music.
    b. French Impressionism.
    c. Russian folk song and dance forms.
    d. American jazz.   [a

17. Harmonically, Hindemith avoided the use of
    a. atonality.
    b. a tonal center.
    c. polyharmony.
    d. simple triads.   [a

18. By birth and training, Igor Stravinsky was
    related to the musical tradition of
    a. Czech nationalism.
    b. Impressionism.
    c. Russian modernism.
    d. Russian nationalism.   [d

19. The folk characteristics in his music
    a. increased over the years.
    b. were strongest in his early years.
    c. were carefully researched for accuracy.
    d. were probably accidental.   [b

20. Among twentieth-century composers, Stravinsky
    was one of the most
    a. predictable in his works.
    b. versatile and unpredictable.
    c. conservative and restrained.
    d. consistent in his development.   [b

DIRECTED LISTENING

Bartók: <u>Music for Strings, Percussion, and
Celesta</u>, Second Movement (Side 10, Band 1)

1. The form of the movement is
   a. sonata.
   b. rondo.
   c. free.
   d. theme and variations.   [a

2. The main theme is
   a. heard after an orchestral introduction.
   b. played by solo piano.
   c. heard after a percussion introduction.
   d. heard at once.   [d

3. The strings and celesta are used
   a. to present melodic material only.
   b. to present melodic and percussive material.
   c. to present percussive material only.   [b

4. Harmonically, the movement is predominantly
   a. tonal.
   b. atonal.
   c. major.
   d. minor.   [a

Hindemith: Mathis der Maler Symphony, First
Movement (Side 10, Band 2)

1. After a short introduction, the movement opens
   with an early German chorale presented by
   a. woodwinds and brass.
   b. strings.
   c. trombones.
   d. full orchestra.   [c

2. While the brasses play the chorale, the strings
   a. play a countermelody.
   b. play chords.
   c. play arpeggios.
   d. remain silent.   [a

3. Prominent solos are played throughout the
   movement by the
   a. flute and cello.
   b. cello.
   c. harp.
   d. flute.   [d

4. The exposition and development
   a. are separated by a short pause.
   b. are joined by a long transition section.
   c. are one and the same in this work.   [a

Stravinsky: "Danse sacrale" from The Rite of
Spring (Side 10, Band 3)

1. Stravinsky's major departure here from musical
   tradition appears in the
   a. melody and harmony.
   b. rhythm.
   c. texture and timbre.
   d. form.   [b

2. During the course of the work, all the orchestral instruments are used
   a. percussively.
   b. traditionally only.
   c. melodically only.
   d. primarily for coloric effect.   [a

3. Melodically, "Danse sacrale" is composed of
   a. three major themes.
   b. one theme and variations.
   c. one major theme broken up into loosely
      connected motives.
   d. a series of short evolving motives.   [d

4. Harmonically, "Danse sacrale" is
   a. never dissonant.
   b. more dissonant than consonant.
   c. occasionally dissonant.
   d. wholly dissonant.   [b

27
Atonality and Serialism

KEY TERMS AND CONCEPTS

Atonality
Serialism
  Twelve-Tone Row
    Basic Forms: Original, Retrograde, Inversion,
      Retrograde Inversion
    Possible Transposition of Basic Forms
  Overall Musical Form Evolved from Use of Row
Other Innovations
  Sprechstimme
  Klangfarbenmelodie Technique
  Hauptstimme and Nebenstimme Markings
  Pointillistic Texture

SELF-TEST

Completion Questions:

1. The word that implies that all twelve tones of
   the chromatic scale are to be treated about
   equally is _____.   [atonality

2. Schoenberg's approach was doubtless influenced by his close association with the _____ movement in German painting.   [Expressionist

3. Schoenberg introduced a melodic style in which the singer does not sustain pitches but slides from one note to another; this is called

   _____.   [Sprechstimme

4. Another of his innovations, in which each note of a melody is given to a different instrument, is called _____.   [Klangfarben-
   melodie

5. The underlying principle of the twelve-tone system is that all twelve tones of the chromatic scale must be given _____.   [equal
   emphasis

6. Since all forms of the row may begin on any level of pitch, there is a possible total of _____ forms of any tone row.   [forty-eight

7. Berg's compositions were based largely on serial techniques, but retained a stronger link than Schoenberg's to the style of the _____ period, through their lyrical qualities.   [late Romantic

8. Berg's greatest work is his Expressionistic opera _____, which was poorly received at first.   [Wozzeck

9. Anton von Webern usually wrote for _____ ensembles and solo instruments.   [small

10. In Webern's works, a single note or a very short motive is often followed immediately by one in another part and in a higher or lower register--a technique that produces a _____ texture.   [pointillistic

Multiple Choice:

11. Atonality was the precursor of
    a. Neoclassical music.
    b. Impressionist music.
    c. serial music.
    d. all of the above.   [c

12. The style of Schoenberg's early works is
    a. Neoclassical, consonant, and structured
       in accordance with eighteenth-century
       forms.
    b. early Romantic, following many of the
       practices of Beethoven and Schubert.
    c. late Romantic, chromatic, but still
       basically tonal.
    d. modern, using serialist techniques.   [c

13. Many of Schoenberg's early atonal works were
    a. songs.
    b. symphonic tone poems.
    c. operas.
    d. concertos.   [a

14. Schoenberg developed the serial system
    a. more or less by chance, as a byproduct
       of his atonal composition.
    b. deliberately as a device to attract
       audiences bored with the older music.
    c. as a musical language to replace the old
       language of tonality.
    d. as a language suitable for use in the
       new electronic medium.   [c

15. Much of Berg's work shows a
    a. serialism even stricter than Schoenberg's.
    b. strongly tonal use of serialism.
    c. serializing of rhythm as well as pitch.
    d. mixture of tonal and atonal harmony.   [d

16. Which of the following is not characteristic
    of Webern's musical style?
    a. Melody that seems to be almost completely
       merged with harmony
    b. A lean and sparse style
    c. Either very small or very wide intervals
    d. Complex, dense texture   [d

Matching:

17. Retrograde
18. Inversion
19. Retrograde Inversion
20. Original

____ the twelve tones of
the chromatic scale
arranged in a row
with none of the
tones used more than
once   [20

____ the original tone row   [19
played back to front
and upside down

____ the original tone row   [18
turned upside down

____ the original tone row   [17
played back to front

DIRECTED LISTENING

Schoenberg: "Mondestrunken" from Pierrot lunaire
(Side 10, Band 4)

1. "Mondestrunken" is scored for
   a. voice, flute, bass clarinet, and viola.
   b. voice, flute, violin, cello, and piano.
   c. voice, clarinet, violin, cello, and piano.
   d. voice, flute, violin, oboe, and harpsichord.   [b

2. The piece opens with
   a. a lyrical melody line.
   b. a short motive heard four times.
   c. three different melodic fragments.
   d. one short motive growing into a second.   [b

3. The form of the song is
   a. strophic.
   b. modified strophic.
   c. free.   [c

4. The stanzas are presented
   a. without a break in the vocal line.
   b. with short instrumental interludes
      between them.
   c. with brief pauses between them.
   d. with long piano interludes between them.   [b

144

Schoenberg: Suite for Piano, Op. 25, First Movement
(Side 10, Band 5)

1. The original tone row is presented by
   a. the right hand.
   b. the left hand.
   c. both hands.   [a

2. The two forms of the row played simultaneously
   near the beginning of the piece make the movement momentarily
   a. change tempo.
   b. percussive.
   c. lyrical.
   d. contrapuntal.   [d

3. Throughout the rest of the movement, various
   forms and transpositions of the row are
   a. heard mainly in inversions.
   b. restricted mainly to the right hand.
   c. used both contrapuntally and chordally.   [c

4. The sense of beat is
   a. clear at all times.
   b. generally obscured.
   c. usually syncopated.   [b

Berg: Lyric Suite, First Movement (Side 10, Band 6)

1. The music is scored for
   a. full orchestra.
   b. chamber orchestra.
   c. string quartet.
   d. wind choir.   [c

2. The main theme is
   a. repeated throughout the movement in easily
      recognizable form.
   b. often hidden in contrapuntal and chordal
      passages.
   c. never repeated.
   d. copiously developed.   [b

3. The strings alternate between
   a. bowed and muted passages.
   b. pizzicato and bowed passages.
   c. muted and pizzicato passages.
   d. pizzicato and tapping the soundboard with
      the fingernails.   [b

4. The form of the first movement is
   a. sonata.
   b. rondo.
   c. free ternary.
   d. free binary.   [d

Webern: Symphony, Op. 21, First Movement
(Side 11, Band 1)

1. The work is scored for
   a. brass and woodwind instruments.
   b. string and brass instruments.
   c. string, woodwind, and brass instruments.
   d. woodwind, brass, and percussion instruments.   [c

2. The melody and harmony are based on
   a. the major-minor system.
   b. the Church modes.
   c. pentatonic scales.
   d. a tone row.   [d

3. A pointillistic texture is created by
   a. the use of great masses of sound.
   b. the extreme delicacy of the sound.
   c. the use of wide leaps within and between
      instrumental parts.
   d. string instruments only.   [c

4. Though the fact is not immediately obvious,
   the first movement is in a free, small
   a. sonata form.
   b. ternary form.
   c. rondo form.
   d. theme and variations form.   [a

Webern: Symphony, Op. 21, Second Movement
(Side 11, Band 1--Immediately following First
Movement)

1. The theme in the second movement is introduced
   by the
   a. horn.
   b. clarinet.
   c. bassoon.
   d. cello.   [b

146

2. The variations are contrasted with one
   another by means of
   a. brief pauses between them.
   b. sharp dynamic changes.
   c. changes in timbre.
   d. changes in key.   [c

3. The tempo is
   a. fast.
   b. moderate.
   c. slow.   [c

4. The string instrument featured in the
   second variation is the
   a. violin.
   b. harp.
   c. cello.   [b

Cumulative Review
Medieval to Early Twentieth Century

SELF-TEST

Matching:

1.	Serialism	___	programmatic piece	[3
2.	Futurism	___	twelve-tone row	[1
3.	Symphonic poem	___	polyphonic vocal work	[4
4.	Caccia	___	third movement in	[10
5.	Polytonality		quick, triple meter	
6.	Leitmotiv	___	recurring motive	[6
7.	Toccata	___	pattern of six equal	[9
8.	Mazurka		intervals	
9.	Whole-tone scale	___	harmonic merging of	[5
10.	Scherzo		varied tonal centers	
		___	noise and microtonal	[2
			music	
		___	early virtuosic	[7
			keyboard piece	
		___	Romantic piano piece	[8
			in $\frac{3}{4}$ meter	

Write M for Medieval, R for Renaissance, B for
Baroque, C for Classical, Rom for Romantic, and
ET for early twentieth century.

___ 11. In the concertato style, performing groups   [B
         played or sang in alternation with each
         other.

148

____ 12. String quartets became very popular.   [C

____ 13. Instrumental music was often related to   [Rom
         extramusical elements such as a story
         or poem.

____ 14. Music was cultivated in the monasteries   [M
         and had an important influence on the
         development of the Church liturgy.

____ 15. From the lute, French harpsichordists took   [B
         over the style brisé.

____ 16. Composers were attracted by the powerful   [Rom
         rhythmic energy of folk music, especially
         dance music.

____ 17. Choral elements were frequently added to   [Rom
         symphonic works.

____ 18. A melodic style was introduced in which   [ET
         the singer did not sustain pitches but
         instead would slide from one note to
         another.

____ 19. A significant trend among composers was an   [ET
         emphasis on objectivity and an attitude of
         detachment from their works.

____ 20. Instrumental music began to be written   [R
         quite frequently for specific instruments.

DIRECTED LISTENING

1. The first movement of which of the following
   string quartets presents a constant polyphonic
   interplay between instruments?
   a. Beethoven's String Quartet No. 7 in F Major
      (Side 6, Band 3)
   b. Berg's Lyric Suite (Side 10, Band 6)   [b

2. Which element is used to create the mood of
   night in both Chopin's Nocturne in E♭ Major
   (Side 7, Band 1) and Schoenberg's "Mondestrunk-
   en" (Side 10, Band 4)?
   a. Tempo
   b. Dynamics   [a

3. The first movement of which of the following
   symphonic works is more concerned with bringing
   out the contrasts of color between the different
   sections of the orchestra?
   a. Webern's Symphony, Op. 21 (Side 11, Band 1)
   b. Hindemith's Mathis der Maler Symphony
      (Side 10, Band 2)   [b

4. Of the following two selections, which has the
   greater rhythmic drive?
   a. Scarlatti's Sonata in C Major (Side 3,
      Band 1)
   b. Schoenberg's Suite for Piano, Op. 25,
      First Movement (Side 10, Band 5)   [a

28
Main Currents in American Music

KEY TERMS AND CONCEPTS

Colonial and Early American Music
  Early Religious Styles
    "Regular" and "Usual"
  Early Developments
    Singing Schools
    Secular Folk Music
    Fasola and Shape-Note Notation
Nineteenth-Century Trends
  Development of Orchestras and Choral Societies
  Dominance of European (German) Styles
  Introduction of Native Elements
    Black and Latin Music
    Band Music
Twentieth-Century Trends
  Nationalism
    Folk Styles and Simple Melodies
    Rhythmic Vitality
  Traditionalism
    Neoromanticism and Neoclassicism
  Progressivism
    Use of New Styles Developed in Europe
  Experimentalism
    Early Use of Polytonality, Polyrhythms, Atonality
    Stereophonic Effects
    Experiments with Piano Timbre

SELF-TEST

Completion Questions:

1. Much of the early musical development in the
American colonies took place in New England,
and was concerned with _____ music.　　　　　[religious

2. A man who claimed to be the first truly
American composer was _____.　　　　　[Francis
　　　　　　　　　　　　　　　　　　　　　　　　　　　　　Hopkinson

3. A system of sight singing popular in the
eighteenth century was known as _____,　　　[fasola
after the three main syllables it used.

4. Perhaps the prototypical American composer
of the nineteenth century was the German-
trained _____.　　　　　　　　　　　　　　[Edward
　　　　　　　　　　　　　　　　　　　　　　　　　　　　　MacDowell

5. One effect of World War I was to turn the
attention of many young musicians from the
German to the _____ tradition, which　　　　[French
encouraged the absorption of new influences.

6. According to Deri's categorization of twentieth-
century American composers, the _____ are　　[Nationalists
those who have attempted to base their work
on American folk styles, especially jazz and
religious music.

7. An important Nationalist composer, especially
notable for his deep understanding of jazz,
was _____.　　　　　　　　　　　　　　　　[George
　　　　　　　　　　　　　　　　　　　　　　　　　　　　　Gershwin

8. The Traditionalists can be divided into two
very different subgroups, the _____ and　　　[Neoromantics
the Neoclassicists.

9. Composers who have developed modern styles,
often based on techniques developed by others,
make up the group Deri calls the _____.　　　[Progressives

10. Among Cowell's most important contributions are his studies of non-Western music and his expansion of the capabilities of the _____.   [piano

Multiple Choice:

11. An early American style of singing religious songs that was often ornate and improvisatory was
    a. the "regular" style of urban church congregations.
    b. the "usual" style of rural church congregations.
    c. the Southern Baptist style.
    d. the black gospel style.   [b

12. Which of the following composers showed traces of Caribbean rhythms in his late Romantic works?
    a. Dudley Buck
    b. John Knowles Paine
    c. Louis Gottschalk
    d. Horatio Parker   [c

13. Which of the following is not characteristic of Copland's style?
    a. Melodies based on folk and religious tunes
    b. Blurred, indistinct rhythms
    c. Predominantly tonal harmony
    d. A transparent texture that stresses individual instrumental timbres   [b

14. Between the Traditionalists and the Experimentalists on the musical spectrum are the
    a. Nationalists.
    b. Progressives.
    c. Impressionists.
    d. electronic composers.   [b

15. Which of the following are not characteristic of the style of Charles Ives?
    a. Polyrhythms
    b. Bitonality and polytonality
    c. Very sparse textures
    d. Tone clusters   [c

Matching:

16. Roger Sessions	___ Nationalist	[17
17. Aaron Copland	___ Progressive	[16
18. Charles Ives	___ Experimentalist	[18
19. Samuel Barber	___ Neoclassical	[20
20. Walter Piston	___ Neoromantic	[19

DIRECTED LISTENING

Copland: Appalachian Spring, First Section
(Side 11, Band 2)

1. After a sustained string note and pianissimo
   clarinet motive, the strings introduce
   a. an eight-measure melody.
   b. a three-note motive.
   c. a theme based on "America."   [b

2. The tempo of the first section is
   a. fast.
   b. moderate.
   c. slow.   [c

3. The mode of the first section is
   a. predominantly major, with some minor
      passages.
   b. minor, with occasional moments of atonality.
   c. not at all clear.   [a

4. In the opening section, the three-note
   motive is
   a. embellished.
   b. repeated, changed, and expanded many times.
   c. repeated only twice in the strings.   [b

Copland: Appalachian Spring, Second Section
(Side 11, Band 2--Immediately following First
Section)

1. The second section opens with a
   a. theme played in rapid, basically descending
      motion.
   b. four-note motive in the horn part.
   c. lyric melody played by the strings.   [a

154

2. The tempo is
   a. fast.
   b. moderate.
   c. slow.   [a

3. Throughout, the music is marked by
   a. frequent changes of meter.
   b. strong reliance on percussive sounds.
   c. ascending and descending arpeggios and
      scales.   [c

4. The section ends with a return to the
   a. slower tempo of the first section.
   b. major mode.
   c. opening theme.   [a

Ives: "Fourth of July" (Side 11, Band 3)

1. As the low strings play sustained chords,
   the opening motive of "Columbia, the Gem
   of the Ocean" is played by
   a. piccolo and flutes.
   b. the wind section.
   c. muted first violins.
   d. cellos.   [c

2. The "Columbia" motive is played
   a. at the beginning of the work only.
   b. intermittently throughout the piece.
   c. at the beginning and in the middle only.   [b

3. The tempo and dynamic level
   a. gradually increase.
   b. alternate between fast and slow, and
      fortissimo and pianissimo.
   c. gradually become slow and softer.   [a

4. The mood changes to a march at the point
   where a solo is played by the
   a. trumpet.
   b. piccolo.
   c. horn.
   d. clarinet.   [b

29
American Popular Music

KEY TERMS AND CONCEPTS

Anglo-American Folk Music
  Simple and Direct
  Major Types
    Ballads, Occupational Songs, Square Dances, Tall Tales
  Incorporation of Some Foreign Influences
Black Folk Music
  Interaction of African and European Elements
  Early Types
    Field Holler, Group Work Song, Ring Shout, Song Sermon,
      Lining Out
  Later Developments
    Blues, Spirituals, Gospel Hymns
  Early Influence on American Culture
    Minstrel Shows and Vaudeville
Jazz
  Emphasis on Syncopation and Improvisation
  Ragtime Precedent
  Early Styles
    New Orleans and Chicago
    Small Jazz Combos
  Big Band (Swing) Style
    New York and Kansas City
    Written Arrangements and Larger Groups

Bop
　　Smaller Ensembles
　　Greater Rhythmic Diversity
　Cool Jazz and Third Stream Jazz
　　More Lyrical Melodies
　　Incorporation of Traditional Musical Elements
Musical Theater
　Operettas and Musical Comedies
Country and Western Music
　Anglo-American and Black Influences
　Western Styles
　　Western Swing, Honky-Tonk, Singing Cowboy
　Other Styles
　　Country Blues, Pop-Country, Bluegrass
Rock Music
　Early Rockabilly
　Rock and Roll
　　Simple and Repetitive
　　Nonsense Syllables and Rhythmic Drive
　Teen Rock
　Beatles and Rock Music
　Other Styles
　　Raga Rock, Baroque Rock, Rock Opera
　　Soul Music
　　Folk-Protest Songs and Folk-Rock

SELF-TEST

Completion Questions:

1. American folk music is rooted principally in
   musical styles from Europe and _____.   [Africa

2. Folk music is generally transmitted by _____   [oral
   means, and in the process it gradually changes.

3. A specialized, ocean-going relative of the
   occupational song is the _____.   [sea chantey

4. An early type of song, often sung by slaves
   working alone in the fields, was the _____   [field holler
   _____.

5. A type of black folk music distinguished by
   lowered thirds and sevenths of the scale came
   to be called _____.   [blues

6. A type of nineteenth-century theatrical
   entertainment, based on the music and humor
   of blacks as understood by whites, was the
   _____.   [minstrel show

7. A late nineteenth-century style related to
   jazz, and inspired by military marches and
   minstrel-show music, was called _____.   [ragtime

8. The most distinctive characteristics of jazz
   are its emphasis on rhythm, especially
   syncopation, and its use of _____.   [improvisation

9. The invention of the _____ was important in   [radio
   helping to popularize country music.

10. The earliest type of rock music was called
    _____.   [rockabilly

Multiple Choice:

11. Which of the following is <u>not</u> characteristic
    of folk music?
    a. Melodies organized into phrases of equal
       length
    b. Rhythm and meter derived from the words
       of the song
    c. A homophonic texture
    d. Asymmetrical and modified strophic form   [d

12. The blending of Euro-American and African
    folk music was possible because the two
    traditions shared
    a. certain characteristics of harmony.
    b. the same rhythms.
    c. the same textures.
    d. similar concepts of timbre.   [a

13. The singers Bessie Smith and Gertrude "Ma"
    Rainey were both associated with
    a. blues.
    b. big band jazz.
    c. traditional jazz.
    d. tin pan alley.   [a

14. Which of the following was <u>not</u> characteristic
    of bop?
    a. Improvisation based on the harmonic structure
       of the music
    b. Increased use of ornamental tones that might
       remain unresolved at the end of a phrase
    c. Little use of chromaticism
    d. Phrases of unexpected lengths and patterns   [c

15. Which of the following is <u>not</u> characteristic
    of country and western music?
    a. Steel guitar
    b. Falsetto singing
    c. Nasal singing style
    d. Lyrics dealing with American frontier themes   [b

Matching:

16. Cole Porter   ____ Annie Get Your Gun   [19
17. George M. Cohan   ____ Oklahoma!   [18
18. Richard Rodgers   ____ Anything Goes   [16
19. Irving Berlin   ____ Babes in Toyland   [20
20. Victor Herbert   ____ Little Johnny Jones   [17

DIRECTED LISTENING

Armstrong: "West End Blues" (Side 11, Band 4)

1. The blues form as used in "West End Blues"
   most closely resembles which of the following
   traditional forms?
   a. Sonata
   b. Theme and variations
   c. Rondo
   d. Fugue   [b

2. The tempo is
   a. fast.
   b. moderate.
   c. slow.   [b

3. Solos are heard in which of the following
   parts?
   a. Trumpet
   b. Trumpet and voice
   c. Trumpet, voice, and clarinet
   d. Trumpet, trombone, voice, clarinet, and
      piano   [d

4. The harmony is supplied mainly by
   a. the piano.
   b. drums.
   c. the clarinet.   [a

Henderson: "King Porter Stomp" (Side 11, Band 5)

1. The meter of "King Porter Stomp" is
   a. duple.
   b. triple.
   c. constantly changing.   [a

2. The timbre is dominated by
   a. percussion.
   b. brass.
   c. woodwinds.   [c

3. The harmony is supplied mainly by
   a. the piano.
   b. drums.
   c. double bass and winds.   [c

4. The form of the piece is
   a. ABA.
   b. AABA.
   c. ABACA.   [b

Parker: "Ornithology" (Side 11, Band 6)

1. The introduction is played by the
   a. saxophone.
   b. piano.
   c. entire combo.   [b

160

2. The music is
   a. basically in the major mode.
   b. basically in the minor mode.
   c. constantly fluctuating between the major
      and minor modes.   [a

3. The tempo is
   a. fast.
   b. moderate.
   c. slow.   [a

4. Solos are played by
   a. saxophone.
   b. saxophone, piano, and trumpet.
   c. saxophone, piano, trumpet, and bass.   [c

30
Music in the Second Half of the Twentieth Century

KEY TERMS AND CONCEPTS

Expansion of Serialism
  Total Serialization
  Intervals of Duration
Electronic Music
  Musique Concrète or Tape Music
  Use of Synthesizers and Computers
New Instrumental and Vocal Techniques
  New Percussive Sounds
  Greater Use of Percussion Instruments
  Use of Speech, Shouts, Whispers, Groans
New Principles of Structure
  Structure Based on Rhythm or Texture
  Aleatoric Music
Music of the Present and Future
  Enormous Variety with Few Accepted Conventions
  Increasing Role for Women

SELF-TEST

Completion Questions:

1. The structuring of each element of music in a
   manner similar to that used in the twelve-tone
   system is often called _____.   [total serial-
                                               ization

2. An influential composer who turned to serialism
   at the end of a long career was _____
   _____.   [Igor
                                                        Stravinsky

3. In the early 1920s, the composer _____   [Edgard
   _____ urged the development of electronic   Varèse
   musical equipment.

4. Because an electronic work can be fully
   realized by the composer, he or she has
   total _____ over the final sound, as   [control
   would not be the case if live performers
   were involved.

5. Most of the development of electronic music
   in the United States has taken place in
   connection with _____.   [universities

6. A composer of electronic music can either
   record and modify natural or instrumental
   sounds, or _____ sounds by electronic   [generate
   means.

7. An important development in contemporary
   instrumental music is the increasingly varied
   use of _____ instruments.   [percussion

8. A strong sense of theater in contemporary
   music has given rise to a number of innovations
   in the techniques of _____ music.   [vocal

9. Cage tried to make his hearers aware of all
   the sounds around them by presenting 4'33",
   sometimes called Cage's "_____ piece."   [silent

10. Aleatoric methods may be used either at the
    stage of composition or at the stage of
    _____.   [performance

Multiple Choice:

11. A composer and teacher of harmony who was
    particularly influential in Paris just after
    World War II was
    a. Arnold Schoenberg.
    b. Béla Bartók.
    c. Olivier Messiaen.
    d. Pierre Boulez.   [c

12. As the term "serial music" is used today,
    it refers to
    a. any piece in which there is a systematic
       ordering of pitches and/or other musical
       elements.
    b. all atonal music.
    c. all music built on a tone row.
    d. any music in which both pitch and rhythm
       are serialized.   [a

13. If a composition requires precise playing
    and exactitude in interpretation to realize
    its full possibilities, it is a good candi-
    date for
    a. the electronic medium.
    b. serialization.
    c. time notation.
    d. aleatoric treatment.   [a

14. An instrument that has especially interested
    modern composers experimenting with new
    timbres is the
    a. guitar.
    b. trumpet.
    c. flute.
    d. violin.   [c

15. When instrumental sounds or sounds from the
    natural environment are taped and modified,
    the resulting music is sometimes called
    a. musique concrète.
    b. musique actualité.
    c. musique verité.
    d. musique nouvelle.   [a

Matching:

16. Karlheinz   ___ Circles   [19
    Stockhausen   ___ First Construction   [17
17. John Cage   in Metal
18. Pierre Boulez   ___ Ancient Voices   [20
19. Luciano Berio   of Children
20. George Crumb   ___ Le Marteau sans   [18
                         maître
                     ___ Zeitmasse   [16

164

DIRECTED LISTENING

Stravinsky: Movements for Piano and Orchestra
(Side 12, Band 1)

1. Melodically, the movements are based
   predominantly on
   a. fragmented motives.
   b. lyrical melodies.
   c. folk-song material.   [a

2. The orchestration includes
   a. mostly unison playing.
   b. many solo passages.
   c. many tutti passages.   [b

3. Rhythms are
   a. heavy with syncopation.
   b. in a clear meter.
   c. polyrhythmic.   [c

4. The movements are separated by
   a. no pause.
   b. a brief pause.
   c. a piano interlude.   [b

Davidovsky: "Synchronisms No. 1" (Side 12, Band 2)

1. The taped sounds
   a. imitate typical flute motives.
   b. are designed to conflict sharply with the
      solo instrument.
   c. are matched with the solo passages in a
      random and aleatoric pattern.   [a

2. Each of the first two sections ends with
   a short passage for
   a. tape alone.
   b. flute alone.
   c. tape and soloist together.   [a

3. The last section is written almost entirely for
   a. tape.
   b. flute.
   c. tape and soloist together.   [b

4. In the first two sections, climaxes are
   achieved through the use of
   a. key changes.
   b. sharp staccato notes.
   c. rubato.
   d. accelerandos and crescendos.   [d

Penderecki: Polymorphia (Side 12, Band 3)

1. The work opens with a
   a. crashing chord.
   b. low sustained sound and a long crescendo.
   c. screeching solo violin sound.
   d. tone cluster.   [b

2. Over the first sound are heard
   a. cello and trumpet solos.
   b. growling sounds in cello and bass.
   c. high, thin, screeching sounds in the violins.
   d. pizzicatos in the violins.   [c

3. Massive blocks of sound result when the
   performers play
   a. glissandi, beginning from the highest
      note on each instrument.
   b. unison chords.
   c. any note of their choosing as loud as
      possible.
   d. quarter tones.   [a

4. The piece ends with a
   a. sustained chord.
   b. pizzicato passage.
   c. muted string passage.
   d. tone cluster reminiscent of Charles Ives.   [a

Carter: Double Concerto for Piano and Harpsichord,
First and Second Sections (Side 12, Band 4)

1. The Double Concerto opens with a
   a. harpsichord cadenza.
   b. percussion introduction.
   c. duet for piano and harpsichord.
   d. series of sustained chords in the winds.   [b

166

2. The first two sections contain
   a. little ensemble playing.
   b. predominant contrapuntal passages.
   c. a theme and variations schema.   [a

3. The solo instrument in the second section
   is the
   a. piano.
   b. harpsichord.
   c. harp.   [b

4. The meter
   a. is predominantly duple.
   b. is predominantly triple.
   c. changes constantly, so that there is no
      strong sense of beat.
   d. clearly alternates between duple and triple. [c

Cumulative Review
Medieval to Present

SELF-TEST

Matching:

1. Synthesizer
2. Prepared piano
3. Celesta
4. Viol
5. Fuging tune
6. Minnesingers
7. The Six
8. Honky-tonk
9. Lute
10. Ostinato

____ instrument developed   [2
    by Cage
____ psalm setting   [5
____ composers of courtly   [6
    love songs
____ constantly repeated   [10
    motive
____ family of string   [4
    instruments
____ instrument that   [1
    manufactures timbres
____ keyboard instrument   [3
    with steel bars
____ writers of light   [7
    and satiric music
____ country western song   [8
    style
____ plucked string   [9
    instrument

Write M for Medieval, R for Renaissance, B for
Baroque, C for Classical, Rom for Romantic, ET for
early twentieth century, and PW for post-World War
II.

____ 11. Two highly successful ballets were   [ET
        The Firebird and Petrouchka.

____ 12. Grand opera presented a production on   [Rom
        a huge scale.

____ 13. Composers tried to make opera seria   [C
        simpler and more emotionally direct.

____ 14. The Florentine operas were comprised   [B
        almost exclusively of monody.

____ 15. Players of traditional instruments became   [PW
        not just interpreters but composers in
        many works that changed at each performance.

____ 16. Much of the symphonic music was meant to   [Rom
        have an emotional impact on the audience.

____ 17. Chromaticism, huge orchestras, and the   [Rom
        addition of choruses to symphonies were
        all very popular.

____ 18. The Venetian style used contrasting   [R
        masses of sound.

____ 19. Polyphonic texture was first widely used.   [M

____ 20. Composers began to use folk material from   [Rom
        various Slavic countries, dance rhythms,
        and pentatonic scales.

_____

DIRECTED LISTENING

1. Two ballet pieces, Stravinsky's "Danse sacrale"
   (Side 10, Band 3) and the first section of
   Copland's Appalachian Spring (Side 11, Band 2),
   differ in that
   a. only Stravinsky stresses percussive sounds.
   b. only Copland makes use of a full orchestra.   [a

169

2. Meter in Davidovsky's "Synchronisms No. 1"
   (Side 12, Band 2) and Armstrong's "West End
   Blues" (Side 11, Band 4)
   a. falls into the same strong duple pattern.
   b. differs in that the first is difficult to
      hear and the second is strongly duple.
   c. is difficult to hear in both pieces.   [b

3. Stravinsky's Movements for Piano and Orchestra
   (Side 12, Band 1) resembles his earlier "Danse
   sacrale" (Side 10, Band 3) most clearly in its
   a. harmony.
   b. instrumentation.
   c. use of short motives.   [c

4. Debussy's Prélude à l'après-midi d'un faune
   (Side 9, Band 4) and Monteverdi's "Tu se' morta"
   (Side 3, Band 5) both achieve much of their
   expressiveness through the use of
   a. strong rhythms.
   b. dynamic changes.
   c. dissonance.   [c